Love A Little

Sherri L. Lewis

&

Rhonda McKnight

~~~

Grace Publications

P.O. Box 514

Stockbridge GA 30281

SHERRI L. LEWIS & RHONDA MCKNIGHT

Jordan Family Series

Give A Little Love (Brooke's story)

Live A Little (Gage's story)

Love A Little (Cree's story)

Dream A Little – Jan 2017 (Arielle's story)

Laugh A Little – Spring 2017 (Cade's story)

Other Titles

When She Loves

A Woman's Revenge

---

iii

Love A Little

Sherri L. Lewis

&

Rhonda McKnight

Table of Contents

Love A Little

Chapter 1

Cree Jordan yawned and raised her hand to her mouth to cover a second long, exaggerated yawn. "Excuse me," she said.

Harrison Lansing or Mansing, whatever his last name was, didn't seem to care. He kept talking.

Okay, so he wasn't the type that was going to take a hint or get offended that she'd yawned while he was telling her all about himself and his super successful business. She was going to have to get right to it in order to end this boring date. She was going to have to go Crude on him – Cree-rude and it wasn't going to be hard. He'd been crass and rude to her twice and he'd treated the poor server like a house slave. She'd given up meanness for Lent, but not justice, so she'd decided it would be her pleasure to ruin his morning.

"I told you I went to Princeton?" He glowered as he raised his fork for the 400th time and shoveled it into that portly hole he called a mouth.

"Three times," Cree replied, tartly. "But only once this morning." She should have known to say no to his invitation when he'd pushed his, "I went to Princeton" last night. She'd met Harrison in the hotel bar after she'd attended a mix and mingle with the other Greeting Card Association

Conference attendees.

He smiled like he thought her humor was charming. His short stubby fingers encircled his glass and he raised it to his mouth. Short fingers. Ugh. She should have noticed those last night.

Harrison looked only a little bit embarrassed about the three times comment. "Right, and where did you go?"

"I didn't."

He frowned.

"I got pregnant my senior year in high school and dropped out to take care of my twins."

"You have children?" he asked like she'd said something nasty or passed gas at the table.

"Four." The lie came easily. She didn't have any children, but the threat often sent men running into the night – or day as it were at this moment.

"Four," he repeated. "Well, I'll be a monkey's uncle. You're quite…"

"Fertile?" she batted her eyelashes and smiled.

"Surprising," he replied. "I like kids. I'm good with them, but I don't have any."

Unable to imagine him being good at anything but eating and being scholarly, Cree shifted in her chair. This breakfast should be over by now. She'd yawned, told him she had four kids and he was still raising his fork and looking at her with interest. How had she gotten herself into this?

Why was she out with this clown?

And then she remembered. Shoes. Last night, she looked down at his Salvatore Ferragamo's and thought about the Louboutin sandals in her luggage. She'd spent all her money and when she was broke, she took meals in from wherever they came. When Harrison offered last night after she'd already had dinner, she suggested breakfast, because the hotel didn't have a free one and she needed to eat before she boarded the airplane. Plus, she rarely turned down a man who wore Ferragamo shoes. She was too impressed with them.

"Harrison," Cree shoved her chair back and stood, "it was really nice getting to know you better, but I have a plane to catch."

"Plane?" He frowned. "I thought you lived here."

"In the hotel?"

He rolled his eyes. "No, I mean Atlanta."

"If I lived in Atlanta, I wouldn't be in the hotel."

"I mean, I thought you lived close enough to have driven to the conference or whatever it was you said you were attending."

"The Greeting Card Association Annual Convention." Cree shook her head. "And I don't know where you got that idea. I never said it."

His disappointment was palpable.

"I should get going. It's an international flight."

"International? So you don't even live in the country?"

Was he daft? Did Princeton graduate such? Of course they did. He wasn't the first overeducated fool she'd had a meal with. She sighed. "I do live in the country," she said raising quotation marks on the word "country" for emphasis. "I'm going to Kenya."

"Africa?"

"It's the only Kenya I know. I don't think there's a Kenya, Florida or a Kenya, Maryland."

He raised his glass and finished his drink. "Why are you going to Kenya?"

"My sister is getting married in a few days and I'm her maid of honor."

"Are you African?"

Cree frowned. Did she sound African? "No."

"Is she marrying an African?"

Cree couldn't imagine why he cared, but she answered anyway. "No, she and her American husband are getting married in Africa."

"Why on earth would they do that?"

Cree rolled her eyes. "I have to go."

He stood now. "Well, wait. What kind of way is that to end our date?"

Cree cocked her head. "How else would it

end except to stop? It's a breakfast date, Harrison. You didn't think you were going to get some did you? It's not even night time. Only people who really like or love each other have sex in the daylight."

He squinted. "I was hoping to get your telephone number."

"So you could become my fifth baby daddy?"

"You have a set of twins, remember? So even if you had four kids, you'd only potentially have three fathers."

"Not if I wasn't sure which of the Clark brothers was the father of the twins."

He smirked. "I can tell by looking at you that you don't have any kids. I suspect you're making up stories to get away from me."

"If you'd gone to Harvard, you'd know for sure."

He pushed his back against the chair. "Have a nice flight, Cree."

She smiled. "You have a nice life." She reached into her bag, removed her cell phone, and walked away from the table. "Jerk," she mumbled to herself as she exited the hotel restaurant. Cree sailed through the lobby and retrieved her luggage from the front desk.

The bellman hailed a taxi and within five minutes she was on her way to Atlanta, Hartsfield

Jackson Airport. Nestled safely in the rear of the taxi, she opened Facetime and called her sisters.

"I can't believe you're not here. We miss you so much, Creesie," Brooke Jordan gushed and swung around so that Cree could see her wedding dress.

Cree gasped. Brooke looked amazing and she couldn't be happier for her. Brooke was getting married. Again. But this time it was for life. This time her sister had found a prince instead of a frog. And the dress…it couldn't be more –

"What do you think of my dress?" Brooke asked, twirling for the second time.

"It's beautiful. You make a beautiful bride. The second time around." Cree wrinkled up her nose. "That first dress was…"

"Cree!" Arielle screeched.

Cree laughed. "I'm teasing." She yawned again. She hadn't been this tired in years.

"You must be exhausted," Arielle said.

"I can't believe you finally start getting serious about your business right before my wedding. How dare you?"

"The conference was great, thank you very much," Cree replied. "I have a meeting with Hallmark's Mahogany Greeting Cards in a few weeks. They want to add a snarky, artistic line to their portfolio. Who could be better for that than me?"

"Sweet!" Arielle raised a hand and gave her a virtual hi-five, which she returned.

Brooke frowned. "I'm happy for you, but I want you here."

"You act like I'm not coming."

"Twenty-eight hours is a whole 'nother day." Brooke poked out her lips like a three year-old.

"Well, at least with my not being there, I'm not getting on your nerves. Be happy about that."

Brooke shrugged.

"So tell me, what are you guys getting into tonight? It's dinner time there, right?"

"Yep. Chase and Pamela took a cooking class, so they're teasing us with a tasting of the food they learned to make."

"Sounds appetizing," Cree said, fully knowing her brother and his wife could nail any dish, no matter what part of the world it originated from. She felt a slight pang of disappointment at not already being there with everyone else in her family. "Don't make me jealous about the food. Tell me, what did you all do today while they were in class?"

"We went on a tour."

"Not a safari?" Cree shrieked.

Arielle dismissed her drama with a wave of a hand. "No, we told you we would do that after the wedding since Brooke and Marcus already did one."

"Are Marcus's cousin's there yet?"

Arielle was quick to reply. "Three of them. And girl, they are fiyah."

"Those Thompsons have some good genes," Brooke added. "I have to give them that."

"His best friend is here too, but he's married."

"So I heard." Cree dismissed thoughts of him. "Well, the cousins are a start."

Brooke frowned. "Isn't that a bit incestuous?"

"Heifer, please, they aren't *our* cousins."

Brooke nodded. "Okay, right. They would need to be ours."

"I thought you were on a man-fast," Arielle interjected.

"I was, but it got hard out there in them streets, so I had to break it."

Arielle and Brooke looked at each other and chimed in unison, "She needed something to eat."

"Don't act like I'm that predictable."

"You are," Arielle said.

"Well, I'm a starving artist, so you know I have to sing for my supper."

Arielle shook her head. "The implications."

"You just have a dirty mind," Cree said. "You need to learn how to keep your coins in your bank account while you build your little business, chickie. You might want to take a lesson from your big sis."

Arielle waved a hand. "I'll let you know when my bank account gets low and you can school me then."

Brooke had stepped out of the conversation and came back into view. She was wearing her veil.

"Awww," Cree crooned. "You look like a fairytale princess."

"I feel like one. Marcus is a prince."

"Yes, he is. You definitely got it right with that one." She leaned forward, put an elbow on her knee, propped her chin on her palm, and sighed. "I hope to meet my prince one day."

"You probably already met him," Arielle said, fanning Brooke's veil out. "But he didn't meet your '4 C' criteria."

"I assure you, I haven't met anyone who was cute, had coin, had good credit and had enough centimeters of height."

Brooke pulled the veil over her face. "Interesting that a Christian woman wouldn't have one of her 'C's' be Christian."

Cree smirked. "Girl, that's on the list. And if he's not, I'll just have to convert him."

Arielle and Brooke gave each other another look.

Cree laughed. "I'm kidding. Don't get all confused in the face."

They chatted about more wedding details all

the way to the airport and while Cree waited in line for the driver to get to the check-in counter. Cree stepped out of the cab and just as she heard the trunk pop, she also heard her name.

"Cree?"

She followed the voice and couldn't believe her eyes. "Wayne?"

She stepped up on the curb, but in her shock she mis-stepped and nearly took a tumble to the ground. The reason she hadn't was because Wayne caught her and now his arms were around her, his face inches from hers.

"I can't believe it. You look like you haven't aged a day." His minty breath was a whisper against her lips.

Cree closed her eyes and swallowed. His cologne was so pungent she nearly tasted it.

"I'm going to get old waiting for my fare," the taxi driver said, closing the trunk.

Cree straightened her back as Wayne pulled her upright.

He released her hand and reached into his pocket for his wallet. "What does she owe you?" he asked the driver without taking his eyes off of her.

"Twenty-three dollars," he replied.

Wayne removed a few bills and shoved them at him. "Keep the change," he said and pulled Cree's bag from the edge of the curb. "You have everything?" He broke their eye contact and looked into the back of the cab.

The spell Wayne had cast broke. Cree looked down at her small carry-on and handbag and then her one piece of luggage and nodded. "That's it."

"You're packing light these days." His voice was teasing. She had a 32-inch Rimowa which was more than big enough for any traveler.

"Who is that?" She heard Brooke's voice coming from her phone. She'd forgotten she'd been talking to her sisters.

"Is that Brooke?" Wayne asked, taking the phone from her hand and turning it to himself. "Hey Brooke," he said, like they were old friends. "How are you?"

Cree snatched the phone out of his hand before Brooke could sneer at him. "I'll talk to you guys once I check in." She ended the call and dropped the phone in her purse.

"Was that a wedding dress I just saw?" Wayne asked.

"I can't believe…of all places…the airport." Cree pursed her lips.

"I know. Look at God." Wayne smiled as he reached for her bag. "What airline are you checking in with?"

"I can get it myself." She pulled it from his hands. "I'm meeting a friend. They should be here any minute."

Wayne smiled that dashing, heart-grabbing smile of his again. He looked like Eric Benet with his bedroom eyes and full, kissable lips. She remembered a time when this man made her insides shift. But his smile and looks no longer worked on her. "It must be a woman or you would have said he."

Cree rolled her eyes.

"What are you doing flying out of Atlanta? Do you live here now?"

"No. I was here for business."

"Cool." He hesitated for a moment like he was thinking about what to say next and then asked, "Why haven't you returned my calls?"

Cree furrowed her eyebrows. "Calls?"

"Don't play. You know I've called you several times in the past few months and I've emailed you."

"I changed my email address."

"I used the one at your website," he said. "And I know I have the correct phone number because your voice is on the message."

She crossed her arms over her chest. "Well, you have my attention now. What do you want?"

"I want to have dinner. We need to talk."

Cree shook her head. "I don't think we have anything to talk about."

Wayne's phone rang and he answered. "Hey, you guys just made it in?" He held up a finger. "Yeah, I'm coming right now." He glanced at his watch. "The flight's not leaving any time soon, so what's the rush?" He listened for a minute then rolled his eyes. "Okay, I'm coming."

Wayne frowned. "Look, I'm traveling with a group. They just arrived from Charleston and I'm meeting them at the gate. The leader is all spastic, so I've got to go. Promise me you'll call me back or I'll miss my flight standing here just so I can talk to you." He raised a hand to her shoulder and smoothed it down her arm.

Even through her jacket, she could feel his warmth. Cree let out a sigh. She hated to promise Wayne anything, but she wanted to get rid of him so she could check her bag and get on her way. She nodded.

He smiled again and leaned in to kiss her on the cheek. "I'm going to call you in exactly eight days and I want a call back or so help me, I'll drive to Charlotte and show up at ya mama's house."

Cree smirked. "Have a good flight."

"You too, Angel," he said. And with that he jetted towards the airport door.

Angel. The term of endearment stirred a storm in her emotions. She'd been no angel when they were together and with the way their relationship ended, he'd become the devil. Dinner with him was an unnecessary journey back down memory lane that she had no desire to take, no matter how much he called.

She pulled the bag along the sidewalk to the check-in stand and reached into her purse for her e-ticket.

After being over-aggressively searched by a mannish looking, female TSA worker, she rode the train to the terminal and then made swift work of her trip to the gate. And that's when she saw him again. Wayne…sitting with a large group of people in the waiting area at a gate two gates down from hers.

She stopped before he saw her and turned her back to the group. Where was he going? And why was he going with all those people?

She backed up to a cell phone charger area and removed her sunglasses from her bag and slid them on. She didn't want to talk to Wayne, but she had almost an hour before her flight was to depart. She raised her glasses for a second and caught sight of his itinerary. Paris. What was he going to Paris for? Why did she care?

They had more than two hours before his flight left. She didn't want to take a chance of him seeing her at her gate and coming over to talk again. Thanks to him, she had the taxi fare, so she decided to duck into a restaurant just down from the gate and hide until her flight boarded.

She lowered her shades and went into a coffee shop, ordered a cup of tea and claimed a seat at an empty table.

Emotions flooded her. She felt that same sick feeling that had kept her in bed for six months after Wayne broke up with her. Back in the day when she used to love with all her heart. But he had put an end to that. It wasn't just the way he dumped her. It was what came afterward that made her sick to her stomach. It was a secret she had never told anyone. Not even Brooke and Arielle. And she told them everything.

When he called her in eight days, she'd ignore his calls just as she had been. He wasn't going to drive to Charlotte and knock on her parent's door. She knew that for sure, so she'd never have to see him or talk to him again. She pushed the pain from the past back into the little pocket in the back of her heart where she'd kept it all these years, took a deep breath and exhaled. She pulled out her phone. She knew Brooke was dying to know about her run in with Wayne.

Just as she was about to dial, the waitress came with her tea. No sooner than she put the drink in front of her did Cree hear her name again. This time the voice that rose above her didn't come from Wayne.

Chapter 2

His dark skin reminded her of roasted chestnuts, and his eyes were cool like chocolate brown, smoky quartz gemstone. The contrast was startling. It always had been. Cree felt light-headed for a moment. It had been almost ten years since she'd looked into those eyes. His eyes. The man she once loved. Her breath caught audibly. Amused that he had taken her breath, one side of his mouth crept up into that boyish, crooked smile he'd perfected. He was already teasing her.

"Cree Ann." His baritone voice was still raspy. The Low Country, Geechie accent that had been faint in college was nearly completely gone now, but she could hear it in the Ann, that he pronounced Aun. The sound made her stomach swish and her heart beat faster. Cree fought the urge to speak God's name in vain.

"David." Her voice was a dry whisper.

He smiled now, fully, like he was pleased she'd remembered his name. As if she could forget. Tall and still lean if not as lanky as he'd been years ago, he fell onto the seat across from her, purposefully, but still casually and cool like he was certain she wouldn't ask him to get lost.

She wouldn't.

"It's hard to believe that you're more

beautiful than you were the last time I saw you."

Cree closed her eyes and shook her head. David Shaw had been the only man she'd ever met in her life that left her speechless.

Her mouth opened the same time her eyes did, but she struggled with words, so she let her manners speak for her. "Thank you." She caught a glance at herself in the mirrored wall behind the espresso, latte and various other machines and thanked the Diva Goddess that she'd taken the time to put on makeup this morning. Or should she be thanking Harrison? She'd done it for her date, because she never wore makeup when she flew.

"What are you doing here," she managed to ask. "Do you live in Atlanta?"

He shook his head.

"Are you still in Savannah?"

He shook his head again. "I'm kind of a nomad these days."

Confused, she frowned. "A nomad?"

"I've spent the last five months or so backpacking around the country. Now I'm going to Africa."

"Backpacking?" she frowned again. Who backpacked in their thirties? She took in his appearance. Well-worn jeans, a Seattle Seahawks t-shirt and an old, leather bomber jacket. He wore sneakers and next to him, a battered, leather backpack. The last time she'd talked to him, he had no idea what he wanted to do with his life. She wondered if that was still the case.

"Tired of the U.S.?" she asked.

"Some days, but that's not really the reason I'm leaving the country. I'm going on a mission trip to Kenya."

Cree tilted her head. "Missions…like evangelism?"

His mouth lifted in that familiar, sexy half-smile again. "Of sorts."

They were quiet for a few moments, each devouring the other with their eyes and then he spoke. "And you?"

"I'm headed to Kenya, too. Not on a mission trip though. My sister, Brooke, is getting married there."

"Does she live in Kenya?"

"Temporarily. She and her fiancé are on a work assignment. They've decided they love each other too much to wait until they get back to the U.S. to get married."

He nodded understanding. "I get it. They can't wait any longer to have legal sex."

Cree squinted. He had them figured out, but how? What did he know about legal sex? She remembered them talking about God every once in a while back then, but he wasn't a committed Christian that believed in celibacy.

"I see you're doing well. Designing greeting

cards and stationary, yes?"

"Well is relative." She raised an eyebrow. "How do you know that?"

He pulled a napkin out of the holder and began to fold it. Avoiding her eyes as he spoke, he answered, "I Googled you."

A trickle of warmth spiraled from her heart down to her belly. "You looked me up?"

He shrugged. "I got nostalgic. I admit to thinking about you from time to time."

Cree's heart locked in her chest. David Shaw...the only person on the earth that was more direct than she. Who would confess to Googling an old love interest? Not even her. She'd never tell him she'd looked for him all over social media.

He continued to fold and quickly made a small bird from the white napkin.

"You're still doing that?" she stated the obvious. Their eyes connected for a moment.

"I can't help myself. I see a paper napkin. I make a bird," he replied.

Cree dropped her eyes to the perfectly formed swan he'd fashioned. She reached for it and then she remembered.

"I hate art, but I'm good with my hands." David Shaw presented a small bird he'd made from the black cocktail napkins he'd been folding.

Cree loved art and couldn't understand how he could possibly have a C in the one class she'd managed to keep an A average in. Cree raised an open palm over the table and waited for him to drop it onto her hand. He hesitated and then took his index finger and traced every line on her palm while never removing his eyes from hers. No one had ever looked at her in such a completely brazen and sexy way. He took her breath away and she struggled to keep her hand from shaking. Then he smiled and dropped the bird.

She swallowed the nervous sigh she'd wanted to release and played with it for a moment, twirling it about by the wing. "I'll keep it forever," she teased.

David shook his head definitively and the smile faded from his face. "No, you won't."

Her heart began to hammer in her chest. "Why do you say that?" She already knew she wouldn't like the answer. Her instinct was confirmed when he deadpanned her with serious eyes.

"Because Wayne won't let you."

And then she remembered him…Wayne…as quickly as David had made her forget.

David sighed. "I can't believe I'm seeing you after all these years. First, I'm on the same mission trip as Wayne, and now I'm seeing you at the airport. What are the chances?"

Cree's eyes almost popped out of her head.

"Wayne is going on a mission trip?"

David chuckled. "He's a minister."

"Wayne is a minister?" She couldn't get her mind wrapped around it. She sucked her teeth. "Must be bootleg then. He's probably stealing everybody's money and sleeping with all the women."

David frowned just enough to be disconcerting. "I don't know about that. And it's not good to speak about a man of God that way."

Cree rolled her eyes. "Man of God? Please. If he's a man of God, then I'm the Queen of England."

David's crooked smiled emerged again. She knew he was no fan of Wayne's.

"So," she continued, "is he a pastor of a church or something?"

"Sort of, but not really. He has an online ministry – on social media. Youtube videos and all those sites people are using these days – what do you call them? Tweety and Facegram and all that."

Cree laughed. No wonder she hadn't been able to find David on social media. A nomad with no Facebook account. Who had he become? And why was he telling her not to talk about a man of God? He was right about that, but she couldn't believe he was saying anything to defend Wayne. She returned her gaze to his. "So Wayne's your new best friend or something?"

David cocked his head. He frowned, but didn't speak.

"I'm not surprised." She kept the disdain out of her voice, but the thought of the two of them being friendly made her sick. "Wayne's seductive like that."

He pinned her with a hard glare. "Wayne and I are not friends." The magic in David's eyes was gone. The melody in his voice suddenly off-tune. Wayne was coming between them. Again. But she couldn't help probing to find out how. She avoided his eyes by raising her long forgotten cup to her lips and took a sip, then returned it to the table before she turned her eyes back to his. "Why are you traveling with him?"

David drummed his fingers on the table and looked from side to side like he was answering questions in a covert operation, or maybe he was just uncomfortable with a discussion about Wayne. "I'm not. I'm traveling with Greater Christian Church. He and I happen to be on the same trip."

"You and he are in the same church?" Again the thought was incredulous. He and Wayne were like day and night, oil and water, good and evil. They could worship the same God, but not with the same pastor. They were too different.

"I'm not a member of Greater Christian. My father was. He paid for the mission trip, but he died six months ago, so I'm going in his place."

Chapter 3

Cree's eyes were wide with shock, searching his face for what? His grief? The grief had already passed. What had once been a cloud that darkened his days was a now a shadow that intermittently floated past the sun. Still, he pressed his lips together and woefully pushed the thought of his father from his mind.

He was sitting with Cree Ann Jordan and until the moment he saw her enter the coffee shop, he'd thought he'd never see her again. He drank her in. The light sprinkle of freckles across her nose drove him to distraction. She had the longest eyelashes he'd ever seen. Could she be more beautiful? He sucked in a deep breath. But the more important question was, was it possible that he still loved her? After all these years, that she would reach into his chest and squeeze his heart again?

His mind darkened at the thought of Wayne. It was a ridiculous coincidence that his seeing Cree again coincided with Wayne being less than four-hundred feet away. This felt strangely like *déjà vu*. He'd been here before – wanting her and being overshadowed by another man. Not necessarily a better man, just a dude who made it first.

She'd called him bootleg. David smiled inside. Bootleg was not favorable and even though he defended his ministry, she was probably right.

"I'm sorry about your dad." She extended her free hand and touched his, gripped it and squeezed. "Do you mind my asking?"

"He had a heart attack." He said it matter-of-factly, but his own heart burned for a moment. It always did when he thought about how his father's life had been cut in half. Healthy, fit, a good man who spent all of his adult years doing good works, dead at fifty-three. It was criminal. He closed his eyes to the thought and then opened them to meet Cree's impassioned stare.

She shook her head and then tilted it and let her eyes speak for her. Her lips mouthed the words, "I'm sorry." He wasn't sure if she said it audibly. He didn't hear it. He was no longer thinking about his father, but those lips. The ones he'd kissed ten years ago and never forgotten.

"I'm okay," he whispered and grinned a little. He looked down at their intertwined fingers, then flicked his eyes up to hers. She must have sensed the intimacy of her hold because she pulled her hand back, wrapped it around her cup and raised it to her lips.

"So, when is the wedding?"

She cleared her throat and took in a deep breath before letting it out and responding. "Saturday."

He raised his eyebrows. "Just a few days."

She continued to sip her tea and then lowered the cup. "My family is over there. Most of them. We've always wanted to see Africa and so when they said they would elope, we decided to make it a family holiday and join them."

"That's nice." And he did think it was. He remembered Cree was extremely close to her parents and siblings and cousins. He was glad that hadn't changed. It was a part of her charm and one of the things he loved about her. His own family was small. His father had a sister with two children. There were other Shaws – an uncle and his family and a first cousin once removed, but no one he kept up with. His relatives had left the south, migrating north after a vicious split over family land, and not looked back. The land they quarreled over was eventually taken in eminent domain by the county for a price that was well below value.

His mother said the stork brought her and claimed she knew not a soul that she could claim as a blood relative. David never believed that story, but accepted whatever secret his mother decided not to share. He had visions of a deathbed confession about who her people really were.

"How is your mother?" Cree interrupted the barrage of thoughts.

"She's well." He felt a smile tip his lips. "I was just thinking about her."

"Is she still in Charleston?"

"She is, and she's still working for the same family."

Cree smiled timidly, but he knew she knew nothing of a mother who was a nanny for rich people. Her family was full of successful entrepreneurs and doctors and lawyers. He loved that she'd never been snobbish about it. He loved so much about her. It was all coming back to him in a flood of heart thumping admiration.

"She must be devastated about your father."

"I'm sure she is, in her way, but I can't tell. My parents had a very strange situation. Her living away six days a week and his time being spent on the island when she was home."

He wanted to move on from the discussion about his parents. It was sad and definitely not sexy. Cree wasn't married and although he'd spent some time on Google trying to find that out, the lack of a ring – wedding, engagement or otherwise meant she was free, or at least she appeared to be.

Cree looked at her watch. "I'll be boarding soon."

"We're not on the same flight?" He'd been hoping that they'd have more time together.

"No, I'm on Turkish Airways." She reached down and picked up her bag from the chair next to her.

When she looked back up, their eyes met. *Just ask her*. He reasoned all she could say was no.

Years ago, he wouldn't have hesitated, but now with a broken heart in his rearview mirror, he was cautious with her. Still, this was his only chance.

"Can I have your number? I'd like to call you."

She smiled coyly. She was blessed with the cutest, sexiest dimples he'd ever seen. She hesitated for a moment, then lowered her head and reached into her handbag. She played in it for a moment and then rewarded him with a business card. She extended it to him, but when he reached for it she didn't let it go. "You didn't ask me if I was involved with anyone."

"I didn't ask in college either." He tugged at the card and was relieved when she released it.

Cree lowered her eyes for a moment and then raised them. "Two old friends catching up?" she asked.

"Of course. We've always been just friends." He put emphasis on *just*.

His cell phone buzzed. He took it out of his pocket and looked down to read the message. The obsessive-compulsive leader of their missions trip wanted everyone at the gate to go over some information about their trip. "I have to go and meet with the rest of the team."

They both stood. David raised a hand and with the back of it swept her cheek. "I really have thought about you a lot over the years," he admitted. She closed her eyes to his touch and it took everything in him not to kiss her.

"I'll call you." He reached down for his backpack and picked it up.

"In eight days." Her reply was smart and he had no idea how she knew he would be gone for that specified time.

"Not if I can get service before that," he replied.

Her lips fell apart like she was going to say something, but then her words got caught in her throat.

"I waited before," he added. "I won't let someone else get ahead of me again."

He turned and walked out of the café. Once he reached his gate, he realized he hadn't said goodbye. It was not a word he used often. He preferred "see you later" or "talk to you soon" because he was superstitious about goodbyes. It was the only superstition he'd never been able to shake. He walked back to the café.

Cree was still standing in front of it, but her head was down. She was doing something with her phone. He stopped, but not long enough to question himself.

"Cree Ann." He'd always loved calling her by her full name. He stepped into her space. Her honey brown eyes met his, and before she could stop him, he kissed her. It was a fast press to her lips, but he made sure it wasn't desperate. She didn't push back, so he drew her to him until her body was flush against his. He kissed her deeper, tilting her head and cupping her face with his hands. She let herself go, just like she had years ago. He enjoyed every moment of her sweetness until she pulled away.

"I'm sorry," David said, raising a hand to run along her cheekbone. "I had to make sure."

Her swollen lips released the words, "Make sure of what?"

"It was as magical as I remembered."

She nodded like she understood. He picked up his backpack and whispered, "I'll talk to you soon." This time when he left the café, he was satisfied.

Chapter 4

Cree's breath had been stolen by her heartbeat, so much so that she could barely answer the stewardess who greeted her as she boarded the airplane. Thirty minutes later, she'd still been so bedazzled by David that she hadn't noticed that the plane hadn't moved. She'd heard the stewardess in the background, but she'd ignored the announcements. Now she wished she hadn't because she wanted to know what was going on. She only had a two-hour layover in Istanbul on her way to Kenya, so the delay was not cool.

She felt some kind of way about flying on Turkish Airlines, but the ticket was cheaper than flying Air France through Paris, so she opted to go that route in order to save money. Brooke was paying of course. It was her wedding, she had the money and Cree was the brokest of all the Jordan children, so someone was always paying for something for her. She was hoping that would change soon.

She'd begged Brooke to let her have the four hundred dollar difference in the flights to add to her savings so she could pay for the GCA conference she'd just attended. And she was glad she had, because if her meeting with Mahogany Cards went well, she'd finally bring her struggling business out of the red and into the black and maybe, just maybe, no one would be paying her way in the future.

She was tired of living in the red. She had been for years. Ever since Wayne. She couldn't imagine the kind of woman she was back then. She'd been living in debt for ten years because of a man that didn't think twice about dumping her when another woman came along. Her sisters laughed about her 4 C's, but she had a good reason for two of them. She would never deal with a broke man again.

Forget about Wayne. She had just seen David.

David…

She raised her hand to her mouth and ran the tip of her index finger over her lips. *Magical*. Yeah, that's what it was. That's what it had always been. Her heartbeat began to speed up again, just thinking about his kisses and his touch. But then guilt washed over her as she remembered how terribly wrong everything went.

She shook her head and looked at her watch. They still hadn't moved. She considered asking the man next to her about the delay, but he was resting with earbuds in his ears. She chose to wait. Ten minutes later, she rang the stewardess and when she came, she asked about the delay.

"There's a mechanical problem with the plane. We'll be making an announcement soon."

"I can't miss my flight in Istanbul. I only have a two-hour layover."

The stewardess frowned, but then plastered on a plastic smile. Cree panicked. She could tell by the stewardess' face that she wasn't going to make it. She couldn't be late getting to Brooke. They had already gotten the dress without her. She was missing all the fun with her family.

Cree's phone buzzed and she reached into her bag to get it. She had a text message from an unknown, South Carolina number.

God brought us back together and this time I'm not letting you go. ~ David

Cree smiled and blushed. David had always had that effect on her. Making her speechless. Making her smile. Making her heart beat so fast, she thought she would die. No man, not even Wayne, had ever made her feel the way David made her feel. Even from the first time they met.

"You must be an art major."

Cree looked over her shoulder into a chocolate brown pair of eyes that were framed in a strong, angular face. His good looks snatched her breath out of her lungs. Gawd, he was fine.

She turned back to her drawing and continued the sketch she'd been working on. She replied, "I am an art major."

"Freshman?" he inquired.

She nodded.

"I'm in your art foundations class. I sit way up in the rafters."

"But you aren't a freshman."

"No, I'm a senior."

"Why are you just now taking art?"

"I avoided it for the past three years, but now if I want to graduate, I need it."

"So, you don't like art?"

"I appreciate art. I'm just no good at it," he said. "You, however, are very talented."

She considered the compliment and looked up at him. "Thank you."

"Do you like science?"

Cree frowned. "Absolutely not."

"I do. I'm a biology major, so maybe you can do my art homework for me and I'll help you with science."

Cree gave him the side-eye. "I'm taking chemistry."

"I'm good at that, too."

She turned to him now and put her hand on a hip. "I'm getting by okay in chem. I don't need to make a deal."

He took a few steps toward her and closed the distance between them. Air left the space. "Well, if you don't need help with chemistry, what can I offer you?"

She was tempted to move away from him, reclaim her space. His presence was strong, overwhelming really, but she stood her ground, put her back in her response. "You can step back out of my personal space."

David Shaw smiled and Cree would swear she saw a flash of light like sparkle and shine like in a toothpaste commercial. Then he took one step back.

The pilot's voice interrupted her thoughts.

"Ladies and gentleman, we're sorry for the delay."

Cree let out a sigh of relief and looked at her watch. If they left right now, she still had a chance of making her flight to Kenya and not spending a night in a strange country like Turkey.

"Our mechanics have tried, but they've been unable to fix the issue they found. We're going to let you deplane while they get another plane. Looks like we'll have another four-hour delay."

Four-hour delay? She'd never make it to Kenya. The man with the earbuds helped her get her carry-on from overhead. She stomped to the ticket counter like an angry nine-year-old. Most of the passengers sat down in the waiting area, seeming to accept the delay. She couldn't.

"Excuse me, ma'am. I need to be scheduled on another flight."

"Ma'am, there's just a delay. We assure you that the plane will be leaving. There is no other flight out today."

Her voice rose. "Then put me on another airline. I have to get to Kenya. My sister is getting married on Saturday and I'm her maid of honor." Without meaning to, Cree started to cry. It was totally unlike her. She would normally throw a fit and give everyone so much hell that they gave her exactly what she wanted. But her emotions were all over the place. She was exhausted from the conference and from hoping and praying for a break for her business. Her stomach was all in knots after seeing Wayne and re-living all their junk from the past. And David…

Tears slid down her face. "You have to help me."

The woman typed on her computer. "I don't think there's anything we can do."

"What's the problem?" That voice again.

Cree turned and there was David, standing there looking like a knight in shining armor. Or actually, an old leather bomber jacket. He took long strides up to the ticket counter. "Cree Ann, you're still here? What happened?"

Through tears, Cree explained everything. David put on a dashing smile for the airline attendant. "I'm on Air France's flight to Kenya through Paris. Can you check and see if there are any seats left there?" Cree had to wonder how often that smile got David exactly what he wanted.

"Hold on a second." The woman typed for a few moments. "There are two seats left. But the cost to change would be $980. Would you like to put that on your credit card?"

Cree balked. "$980? Sure. Let's just put that on my credit card. Do I look like I have an extra G sitting around to pay for a flight I've already paid for? I booked this flight trusting that you would get me to Kenya on time to prepare for my sister's wedding and now you want to tell me that to get me there on time, I have to pay $980?" The tears were gone and Cree was in full Cree-rude mode. She'd get back to her Lenten vow after she was on a plane to Kenya. "I need to speak to your manager…NOW."

David pulled out his wallet. "It's okay. I'll pay for it."

Cree's mouth fell open. *He'd pay for it. What?* How does a nomad backpacking around the country and going on mission trips pay for a thousand dollar plane ticket? Once again, he had rendered her speechless. She wanted to scream, no, that she couldn't accept that kind of gift from a man she had dumped years ago, but nothing came out.

The woman's phone rang just as she was about to accept David's credit card, giving Cree time to find her words.

"David, I'm grateful that you would be willing to do this for me, but I can't accept it. And I can't pay you back. Like ever."

The woman hung up the phone. "No need. The flight was just cancelled. We have to reroute everybody. Let me get that seat for you before it disappears."

Cree let out a deep breath. God was looking out for her. As always. She was glad she had been the first person at the counter, otherwise, she surely wouldn't have gotten one of the two available seats. She'd make it to her sister's wedding and that's all that mattered. Well, that and the sexy dimple in David's cheek that caught as he smiled at her.

A crowd of people swarmed the counter after the attendant put up the cancelled flight sign. David placed his hand in the small of her back to guide her a few feet away from a large family whom didn't observe the rules of proximity.

David's hand in her back, a simple gesture, one could reason…good old-fashioned, southern manners, but all she could think about was that kiss an hour ago. Just this morning she'd told her sisters she wanted her prince. She stole a sideways glance at David and thought, *"Lord, this ain't no time for jokes."*

Chapter 5

David resisted the urge to do a fist pump and instead pressed his hand into the small of Cree's back. It almost killed him to see her crying and he would have paid any amount of money to make her happy. He would have gladly spent $980 to spend the next twenty hours with her going to Kenya. God had given him the break he needed and he was going to do everything he could over the next few hours to win her heart again. That was assuming he'd actually had it the first time. He wasn't sure.

A thought occurred to him. He leaned and whispered into Cree's ear, "I'll meet you at the gate. I need to take care of something."

She was too happy to notice he was leaving and just gave a little wave.

David rushed back to the ticket counter at Delta and prepared his megawatt smile for the agent at the counter. "I need a seat change please."

It took Cree longer than he'd expected to get her new ticket taken care of. The flight to Paris started boarding. Just when he was about to go check on her, she came rushing up to the gate. Her face was flushed, probably from the tears and then the excitement. She'd taken her mass of loose, unruly curls and twisted them into a bun.

She looked around from left to right, probably looking for Wayne. He didn't know what had gone down between them, but whatever it was had left her sour. That would be to his advantage. He also wasn't sure of the look that crossed her face when she spotted him. Was it relief? Joy? Shyness? It was some version of happy, so he'd take it.

"This worked out well. I'm glad you'll make it to the wedding." He didn't say how glad he was to be able to spend more time with her, but she could probably see it on his face. "You got your seat assignment?" He tried to say it as innocently as possible.

"Yeah. It's a middle seat. I hate middle seats, but I'm grateful just to be on the flight."

They slowly shuffled onto the plane. They passed by Wayne sitting in first class. David shook his head. Who flew first class on a mission trip? Wayne's mouth fell open when he saw Cree. She walked past him like she didn't even see him. Made David want to know what had gone south between them even more. David raised his eyebrows and gave Wayne a triumphant nod as they passed by. It was his turn to get the girl.

When they got to Row 34, Cree looked up and stopped. "This is me."

David made a big show of looking down at his boarding pass. "Huh, well what do you know? I'm here, too." A broad grin spread across his face.

She stared up into his eyes, her eyes first registering shock and then realization. "Yeah, what a coincidence."

He smiled and took her carry-on and pushed it into the overhead bin. "*Merveilleux*."

She squinted. "I took Spanish. What does that mean?"

He replied, "Wonderful."

A group of kids rushed past Cree pushing her close and tight into his body. Instinctively, he raised a hand to her back as if to catch her. Having her warmth next to him twice in the same day was disorienting and exhilarating. She seemed to have sensed it as well because she pushed back from him.

"I would give you the aisle, but my legs won't make it on this long flight."

She shook her head. "The center is fine. Like I said, I'm happy to be on the flight."

Cree plopped down in her seat and David followed and sat next to her. Gold bangles jangled on her small wrist. She leaned forward and slid out of the denim jacket she was wearing.

"Do you want to put that overhead?" he asked.

"I'll hold it. I might get chilly."

"Not likely around me. I've been told I'm like a furnace."

Cree gave him a side-eye. "Who told you that? One of your harem girls?"

David chuckled, leaned forward and turned his head to face her. "Me? A harem? You know me better than that."

She shook her head. "I don't know you at

all."

"No?"

"It's been ten years."

He let out a long breath, continued to hold her gaze for a moment before turning his head forward staring at the seat in front of them. "In some ways, it feels like yesterday."

Cree was quiet for a second, but he could feel her eyes on him as she spoke. "What feels like yesterday?"

He turned back and locked his eyes on hers. "You do."

He saw her swallow hard before she looked away.

Moments later, a petite woman joined them. They both stood to let her into the window seat. She said a cordial hello and popped her headphones in.

"Good. She won't be talking my ear off," Cree said, pulling her phone from her bag. She raised her eyes to his and said, "I got your text."

"I meant it."

"Is that how we got seated together?"

"I might have had a little something to do with that," he confessed easily.

She smiled, but then he realized he wasn't the only one who had been smart enough to hatch a plan. The stewardess stopped on their row and she had Wayne behind her. She waved at the woman in the window seat to get her attention. The woman took her earbuds out.

"Excuse me, ma'am. This gentleman is the lady's fiancé. He's offered to switch seats with you in order to sit with her."

The woman looked at Cree and then David and frowned like she didn't believe it.

"The seat is in first class," Wayne added over her shoulder.

The woman didn't hesitate. She popped up and said, "It's all yours."

Cree sighed audibly as they all stood to let the woman out and Wayne into the window seat.

"David," Wayne said. "I see your luck has changed over the years."

David didn't even try to harness his irritation. "Not really. I still keep running into you."

"Uh, dudes…" Cree interjected. "We're not doing this."

David let out a deep breath. How was he going to win Cree back with Wayne there? Even though Cree was in the middle seat, it felt like Wayne was sitting between them. The guy had a knack for messing up his game when it came to her.

He had planned eight hours of talking, maybe watching an in-flight movie, and anything else she'd let him get away with on a plane. By the morning, she'd be his. His whole plan was shot. He'd have to wait until their flight from Paris to Kenya.

He could only hope that he'd be able to get them seated together again. Without Wayne.

Chapter 6

Cree looked at David on her right and then slowly turned to Wayne on her left. Seriously God? Like, for real??? Was this really happening? Was she really about to spend the next eight hours sitting between the only two men she had ever loved in her life? One who had broken her heart and the other whose heart she had broken? The air was too thick, too intense, and for a moment, she felt like she couldn't breathe.

Her grandmother always said everything happened for a reason. What reason could God possibly have for sitting her between these two? Too many emotions ran through her head and her heart. Towards Wayne – anger, hostility, and resentment. Towards David – regret, intense attraction that somehow was stronger than it had been when they parted ways years ago and...what was she feeling? Fear. Yeah, heart-gripping fear.

She waved to a passing stewardess, "Um uh, when do you guys start serving drinks?"

Cree knew her face must be looking crazy because the stewardess laughed. "Not until we're up at 10,000 feet, ma'am."

Wayne frowned at her. "Baby, you don't drink, do you? Or at least you didn't when we were together." Was it her or did he throw the words "baby" and "together" in David's direction?

"A lot has changed in the last ten years, Wayne." Then she said under her breath, "And if I didn't drink, this would be a good day to start."

She needed to distract herself. She needed to go to her happy place. She pulled her iPad out of her handbag and opened pictures of her artwork. Renderings of flowers and garden scenes that encased open sketches of scriptures. She could feel David watching.

"Is that your work?" he asked.

She turned her head toward him a little and smiled and nodded.

"What are they for?"

"I'm putting together a coloring book."

"For adults?" he asked. "I heard those were popular."

"They are, but there's a lot of competition. I've been working on this one for a few months."

"I think it's sweet that you're still doing your art thing, babe. That's cute." Wayne's voice interjected. "But how are you going to sell a coloring book for grown-ups?"

She tilted her head in his direction. "They sell themselves, actually. The good ones do."

Wayne shrugged and pulled out a tablet of his own. "If you say so. I'd buy a bunch of them and give them to my nieces."

Cree rolled her eyes. He'd never supported

her passion for art.

"Baby, is this what you do for a living?" Wayne asked. "Or do you have a real job too?"

"Are we on a plane or is this a time machine? I haven't been your baby for ten years."

David chuckled as he reached toward her tablet. "May I?" he asked and she handed it to him.

He swiped the screen and watched her creations go by one by one. She could tell he was impressed with her talent, just as he had been all those years ago. She interrupted him. "A few of them are digital images." She pointed. "Like that one."

He turned the iPad sideways. "Hard to tell."

"I do my own renderings, but I play around with technology." She paused. "The fine coloring book connoisseurs prefer hand drawings."

"I read that," he said handing it back to her. "You have a lot of pictures there. You should be ready to go with it. Only takes about thirty, right?"

She furrowed her eyebrows. "Now you know too much."

"I follow Cree's Concepts," he said, referring to the badly neglected blog on her website.

Her lips fell apart and then she closed her mouth. He'd more than Googled her and he obviously wanted her to know it. He'd taken her words again. She was shocked. She stared into his eyes. Why? Why was he Googling her and following her blog? Could it be that he wanted –

Wayne cleared his throat loudly. "Still stalking women?"

David didn't even look up from the iPad when he replied. "I'm not the one that has to stalk women. That's your M.O.."

"Dude, please, I have to send the women away."

"You send them away all right. With your – "

The pilot interrupted, announcing that the plane was about to take off. They all fastened their seat belts. Cree closed her eyes and said a silent prayer of thanks that she was on her way to Kenya and to Brooke, but also asked God to help her through the next eight hours.

As soon as they got up into the air and the roar of the engines calmed down, the men were right back at it.

Wayne started, "I shoulda traded my seat with you, David, instead of that woman. That would have given me and my angel, Cree, a chance to get reacquainted."

"If you had handled your business right the first time, you wouldn't have to get reacquainted. You would have held on to the best thing that ever happened to you when you had her. Don't think I'm going to walk away this time so easily."

"You'll walk away because I'm going to –"

"I'm sitting right here. Right here." Cree huffed. "What are we, sixteen? This is the last time I'm going to say it. If you two grown men don't stop this bickering over me like I'm invisible, I'm gonna throw a panic attack and get moved to first class. Or better still, I'll fake a seizure and they'll turn this whole plane around and we'll go back to Atlanta. I'll fall right out in the aisle and start shaking and drooling." Cree rolled her eyes back in head and stuck her tongue out and shook her whole body.

David chuckled.

Wayne grimaced like the thought disgusted him. "You wouldn't."

"You keep acting like you know me. If you do, you know I would."

Wayne clamped his lips together, obviously realizing that she was crazy enough to do it.

"Now both of y'all sit there and be quiet. Put your headphones in and watch a movie or something. Go to sleep. I don't want to hear another thing from either one of you. Not a word."

Both men obeyed. Wayne put on expensive looking, Bose headphones that he must have paid a mint for. Cree put on her Beats. Well, actually her brother Drake's Beats she had sorta borrowed. Okay, stolen. David put in the cheap headphones provided by the airline.

A few seconds later, David took his out.

"Fake a seizure and go back to Atlanta? As happy as you were to get on this plane and as bad as you want to get to your sister's wedding?"

Cree laughed. "I know, right?" She turned serious. "Please, can you not –"

"I know. I'm sorry. I don't understand why I let him get under my skin like that. This can't be easy for you. I promise to be the bigger man if he starts again."

Cree batted her eyelashes. "Thank you." And she knew he would. Just like he had years ago. Even with all the hell she put him through over Wayne, he had always been the perfect gentleman. David stared at her and she felt herself getting lost in his eyes. Who knows what would have happened if Wayne hadn't busted up their little party? "I miss talking to you."

David smiled. Was he blushing under that dark skin of his? "Me too. I've never had conversations with any woman like I had with you."

"Of course you haven't. How could you? I'm Cree. There's no other woman like me."

They both laughed. That's how they had always been with each other. Blunt and honest. Straight, no chaser. No games. As real as they could be. Which was why it had probably been so easy to love him. She could be fully her, without having to censor herself and he loved every minute of it.

Wayne turned toward them and frowned. He

pulled off his headphones. "Hey, I thought we weren't allowed to talk to you. How come he gets to?"

"Because the sound of his voice doesn't make me want to claw my eyes out," Cree snapped a little more than she meant to. "I don't want to talk to you, Wayne."

He pouted like a five year-old kid. "I gave up my seat in first class to sit back here in economy with you. Do you know how much an international first class ticket costs?"

Cree snapped her head all the way back. "Are you actually talking to me about what something cost?"

Wayne shook his head sheepishly.

"If you wanted to give it up, you should have let me sit up there. Then you guys coulda fought and bickered the whole trip. But I didn't ask you to give up your seat so don't go throwing it in my face like you did me a favor."

"But I thought we could finally talk. You've been ignoring my calls and emails so I figured we could…"

He was doing that whining thing that used to get on her nerves so bad. Big man on campus turned into a little whining punk when he wanted something.

Cree raised her hand and gave her index finger a firm wag. "Uh, uh."

He shut his mouth like he remembered all the arguments they'd had about his whining back in the day.

"Wayne, we have nothing to talk about."

"If you'd just give me a second, you'd see that we do." He lowered his voice to a whisper, "Please. "

Cree rolled her eyes and let out the loudest, most annoyed sigh she could. She gestured toward David to put his headphones on.

David's eyes widened. "Seriously?"

"It'll just take a minute. Really."

Wayne frowned. "When you hear what I want to talk about, you'll realize we need longer."

Cree's eyes dropped to her watch. "You have five minutes."

"Five? That's not enough time to –"

"Four minutes, fifty seconds. Tick tock, tick tock."

Wayne sighed. "I just wanted to…I needed to say that…back when we were together…"

Cree hadn't taken her eyes off her watch.

"Cree, you know I can't talk with you timing me." Wayne's voice was a little loud for a plane. "You know I need your full attention."

She knew that all too well. She had decided near the end of the relationship – the first end – that Wayne was a narcissist, incapable of loving anyone but himself. He needed worship, not love.

Cree released a deep breath and rested her hands in her lap, covering her watch with her right hand. "What, Wayne?" She didn't even try to keep the irritation out of her voice. "Skip the hemming and hawing and say what you got to say."

"I'm sorry. I'm sorry for what happened between us. I...I handled things badly. I hurt you. You...you were good to me. Better than good. Better than I deserved. I owe you an apology."

"Okay."

Wayne looked like he was waiting for her to say something else. He'd be waiting until Jesus came.

He frowned. "Okay? That's all you have to say?"

"What do you want me to say?" Cree felt her temper starting to rise. "Oh. I forgive you. Feel better?"

"Wow. I must have really hurt you."

Had he actually put the word "wow" in front of "I must have really hurt you?" She felt like he'd hit her...knocked the wind out of her. He didn't know the half of it. He didn't know how she had sold her soul to the devil for him. How she had lost a piece of herself when that relationship ended. She never told him the extent of the damage. He didn't know and he never would.

The slight grin on his face made her sick to her stomach. Was he happy that he had hurt her that much? "No, fool. It's just that I find you pathetic. Quite pathetic. You think that after all these years I even care to hear your apology? Just shows how self-absorbed you are."

She drew away from Wayne and leaned in to David. He must have felt her shaking. He jerked off his headphones. "You okay?"

The care and concern in his eyes sent Cree's emotions reeling. This moment with the two of them was too much.

"I'm fine." She slid her headphones back on and started scrolling through the recent movie releases. She had to calm herself down because she was jabbing the chair of the person in front of her, trying to find a decent movie to take her mind off her past.

She felt Wayne tap her on the shoulder. She pulled her headphones off the ear next to him.

"I wasn't done."

"Oh, but you were." Cree slid the headphones back on and leaned back in her chair.

Wayne pulled a pen out of the breast pocket of what had to be a thousand dollar suit. At least. He scrawled something in big letters on the travel magazine from the seatback in front of him. He passed it to Cree. She squinted to read his bad handwriting.

I owe you more than an apology. I want to pay back the money.

She took off her headphones. "I guess you weren't done."

"It's why I've been trying to reach you. I'm trying to make things right from my past. One of them is apologizing to you. And paying back the money."

Cree's pulse sped up. This time it wasn't from hurt or annoyance. *Pay back the money.* Her heart beat a rhythm of cha-ching, cha-ching. "You have my full attention."

Wayne leaned over and looked at David who was quietly watching Matt Damon in a Bourne-something movie. "Not here. I'm not going to whisper on this plane." Wayne knew he had her attention. His confidence was back. She could hear it in the smooth tenor of his voice.

Cree resisted the urge to roll her eyes. She silently counted in her head the money she had spent that year on Wayne. If he paid her back, she could pay off the last bit of debt that was strangling her. She could be free. She could invest in her business and shop without feeling guilty.

"Okay, when and where?"

"Have dinner with me in Kenya. I can come to you. I know you'll be there for Brooke and Marcus Thompson's wedding. Maybe I could come to the rehearsal dinner or something. I could even be your date for the wedding."

Cree took a deep breath and counted to ten.

Otherwise Wayne would have gotten the worst cussing out of his life. "How do we go from you paying back the mountain of money you owe me to you being my date for Brooke's wedding? Do I look like I'm desperate for a date for the wedding? How do you know I'm not meeting my date there?"

Wayne looked around. Cree was a little loud. She lowered her voice into a fierce whisper. "Look, if you want to pay me back, pay me back. I can send you an email with the amount and my payment information. You can deposit it into my account. I don't see why we need to have dinner."

He brushed his hand against hers. "For old time's sake, Angel. I know you don't believe it, but I'm a changed man. If you give me a chance, you'd see that. We were good together. Remember?"

"Remember?" Cree let out a strangled laugh. "I'll tell you what I remember. I remember…" She took a deep breath. Let it out real slow. "I'm not going there with you. You're not worth it. I'll say it again, if you want to pay me back, pay me back. If you're using the money you OWE me to try to work your way back into my life, you can forget it. I'll stay broke." She hadn't meant to say that.

"Are you broke, baby? No need for that. I've got enough to take care of you – well. And I've got a lot more than that gypsy you're sitting next to. I could buy you a house, a car, a new wardrobe – you know how much you love shoes and clothes. I could–"

Cree didn't hear another word because she put her headphones back on and turned her movie up until it hurt her ears. A few seconds later, the stewardess passed by with the drink and snack cart, headed toward the front of their section.

She took off her headphones. "Girlfriend, help a sistah out. Do you have anything with chocolate…some covered pretzel or something?"

The woman chuckled. "I got you, girl." She reached way back into the bottom of the cart and pulled out a bag of M&M's.

Cree clapped and then accepted the bag. Another passenger said, "I'd like a Bloody Mary, please."

The stewardess frowned. "I'll be back to your row in a minute, sir."

"But…" The man turned to look at Cree and back at the stewardess. Both gave him attitude – side-eye with lips pursed, daring him to say anything else. He settled back into his seat. The stewardess winked at Cree and kept rolling to the front.

Cree replaced her headphones. Opened the bag, planning to savor them. Wayne tapped her on the shoulder and then reached his hand over to remove the headphone on his side.

He whispered into her ear, "Remember the times when we were good together. We could be good again. And I'll take good care of you. Like you took care of me and like you deserve to be taken care of. Just think about it."

"Never. Now leave me alone."

"Baby, don't be like that."

"If you call me baby one more time, I'm gonna punch you in the throat." She pushed his hand away and put her headphones back on.

She propped her pillow behind her head and spread her blanket over her legs. They had gotten to a high enough altitude that it was a little chilly. A few minutes later, she felt David's hand under her blanket, squeezing her knee. She knew he was trying to comfort her and make sure she was okay after dealing with Wayne's foolishness. It was sweet of him to want to calm her down, but he was having the opposite effect. His big, strong hand on her knee sent heat rippling through her entire body.

She gave him a weak smile and playfully pushed his hand off her knee. He winked at her and gave her that sexy smile. Her heart took off racing.

She had eaten half the bag of candy. By the time the stewardess came back to their row, she'd be ready for another bag. She hoped girlfriend had one.

Chapter 7

Thirty-thousand dollars.

Cree tried to focus on the movie playing on the screen in front of her, but all she could think of was thirty-thousand dollars. Thirty-thousand dollars. If Wayne gave her back the money, she'd have enough to finish paying off her student loans and still have some left over since she'd been paying them for a while.

They had eaten their airplane food dinner that actually tasted pretty good. Wayne was sulking and playing a game on his tablet. David was watching a movie, but sneaking glances at her. They had both been peaceful, so she kept her earphones on, even though she wasn't listening to the movie, hoping that her earphones would keep them silent.

Cree glanced down at Wayne's words scrawled on the travel magazine. "I want to pay back the money." She had never thought of trying to recover the money from Wayne, but it was only fair. He owed her.

They'd been dating for a year when everything happened. The first six months were a whirlwind romance. She was attracted to his magnetic personality. He was Student Council President so she wasn't the only one that found him dynamic. He could talk a turtle out of its shell with his charismatic ways. And with his good looks, the women were always gathered around him. But he chose her – he was a junior and she was a newbie freshman on campus.

Their relationship was very public and she loved being the center of attention as his girlfriend. But six months in, things started going bad. His charisma and charm were masks for his insecurities. In public he was gregarious and lovable, but in private, he was self-centered and honestly, a jerk. They started arguing all the time and by month eight, Cree was ready to get out of the relationship. She met David right at the end. The first end.

She'd fallen totally head over heels for him. He was everything Wayne wasn't. Where Wayne was outspoken and social, David was quiet and thoughtful. Wayne lived out loud while David was intensely private. And where Wayne was childish and insecure, David was the strongest, most self-assured person she'd ever met. The choice was easy. Until…

"You can't break up with me, baby. I'm sick."

"Sick? Whatever, Wayne. This is just another one of your sick tricks, trying to keep me trapped in this relationship. I'm tired of your manipulation and your games. Feed it to someone else."

"Angel, I know I've been terrible to you. And I know you have no reason to believe me. But it's true. I have brain cancer."

Cree laughed out loud. "Brain cancer. You think I'm an idiot? How pathetic that you would fake cancer to keep me from breaking up with you. Who does that?"

But her heart stopped. The voice in her head said...the headaches.

Wayne shook his head. "You know those headaches you told me to go get checked out?"

Cree nodded.

"Well I did." Wayne walked over to his desk and removed out a large envelope. He pulled out a large X-ray film and a folder. "Here. This is my MRI and all the tests they've ordered for me to do next." He held up the MRI for her to take.

She just stood there. "You're serious?"

He gulped and nodded.

Cree gasped. She listened to him talk about his prognosis and percentages and treatments, but it was all a blur. Wayne...cancer. How could this be? He was too young to be sick. As much as she was tired of Wayne and his crap, she didn't wish the worst on him. She had loved him. "I'm...sorry. That's awful."

He moved into her space. "I'm sorry. For everything. You know I don't mean to be this way. In fact, they said that some of the personality changes might be because of the cancer."

Cree shook her head. It was too much to take in.

Wayne pulled her into his arms. "You know I really love you. Please...don't leave me. I need you. They're talking chemo and radiation. I can't do this alone. You know I don't have anybody but you."

That's where he got her. Six months into their relationship, he had taken her to his little hometown in Jenkins County, Georgia. She had understood him that day. The insecurity. The grandiosity. Wayne had grown up dirt poor in a little town that you'd miss if you blinked passing through. Somehow he had beat all the odds and made something of himself. He was the first of his small family to go to college.

Cree had always loved being a part of her big, supportive family. She didn't understand a family that was always at each other's throats. That day when they left his town, her heart went out to him. She decided she would love him and she would be his family.

He reminded her of that day. Of that promise. "Don't leave me, baby. Please, I need you."

And so she had opened her heart to Wayne and stayed. She'd shut down her heart to David.

Refused all his calls and told him she was staying with Wayne. She never gave him any explanation. Wayne had sworn her to secrecy. She thought saying nothing was better than a lie, so she just left David wondering why.

She went to every chemo and radiation appointment with Wayne. She held the trashcan for him when he vomited. She eventually moved in with him and did the grocery shopping, cooked all his meals, and kept the apartment clean. She held him all night long when he woke up from nightmares about dying. She even gave him her body for comfort, even though the Jordan girls believed in waiting until they got married. *She* believed she would wait until marriage.

One month after the doctors had pronounced that his cancer was in complete remission, when they should have been celebrating his life, he broke up with her. He dumped her for some high society chick from Atlanta whose parents had a lot of money.

Cree felt her anger rise again. How had she been such a fool? Why had she given so much to someone who had given her so little? And then there was the money. All that money. She pushed it out of her mind like she had for nearly ten years. She didn't want to remember the crazy mistake she had made that she was still paying for. She was just glad there was a chance she could get it back.

She shoved more candy in her mouth and fought letting the rising tears fall. She would not let him see her cry.

She stole a peek at him. It was only right that she got that money back. Maybe it was God that orchestrated them sitting next to each other on the plane. God knew she was struggling and knew the sacrifice she had made in the past. He wanted to give her this chunk of money so she could get the debt monkey off her back and invest in her business.

Wayne giving the money back was justice. And she was all about justice. And if she could put up with breakfast with Harrison Lansing for a $30 meal, surely she could stomach breakfast with Wayne to get her $30,000 back.

She took off her headphones and leaned in Wayne's direction. She hoped David's cheap airline earphones would keep him from hearing.

Wayne took off his headphones when she tapped him on the shoulder. "Yes?"

"We have a three-hour layover in Paris. I'll have breakfast with you then."

His face broke out in too wide of a grin. He looked triumphant. "Okay, baby. That sounds good."

She started to correct him for calling her baby again, and to tell him to wipe that stupid grin off his face, but she'd play along. She wanted her money back and she'd do what she needed to do to get it. She patted his leg and put her headphones back on.

Wayne must have been happy with her answer because a few minutes later, she looked over and he was asleep. He always did catch the "itis" and drop off after he ate. And unless something had changed, he slept like the dead.

David leaned past her and looked at Wayne. "I thought he'd never go to sleep." He removed his headphones and then hers. He lifted the armrest between them and took her by the hand. She felt the electric current passing from his hand to hers and it sent jolts through her whole body.

"Now catch me up on the last ten years of your life."

"Just like that? I'm supposed to tell you the last ten years of my life?" Cree couldn't stop the smile that filled her face. He had always made her smile. Every moment with him up until their last had been filled with joy.

"Yes, ma'am, I want to know what you've been up to."

Before she knew it, Cree had talked almost an hour straight. And David hung on her every word. Like she was the most interesting person on the planet. He had a way of staring at her when she talked that made her feel like he was seeing her soul through every word. It made her high.

Every so often, he would brush her face with his hand, or squeeze her knee. He was completely into her, but she knew she had talked too long when his eyelids started to droop.

"Look at you. You're sleepy."

"No, I'm not. I'm listening." He smiled at her with closed eyes.

This always happened to them. Whenever they got together, they stayed up half the night talking. She was exhilarated by his presence and got more energetic as the night passed. She always said that she bored him and that's why he was the first to fall asleep. But he told her that she gave him peace. That he felt like he could really rest when he was around her. She made him feel like home. Like his mama's gumbo, jalapeno cornbread and a tall glass of milk on a rainy day. The thought of that made her smile. He was so low country. But the idea that she made him so calm that his soul could rest and sleep better made him feel like home to her.

She had never had sex with him. She and David would talk, with her doing most of the talking, until he fell asleep in her arms. Then she'd lay there for a while and think until she fell asleep. And like Wayne, he slept like the dead. At least when she was around.

David took a finger and traced her eyebrows, down her nose, around her lips. His finger trailed down her neck and then back up to her lips again. The whole time, he stared at her with desire in his eyes. He still wanted her after all these years. It was like time had stood still. Cree felt herself getting dizzy. From the finger, from the look in his eyes. Just when she thought she couldn't take it anymore, he leaned in to kiss her. Soft and sweet, like feathers brushing her lips. She got lost in his eyes and had to remind herself that they were on a plane. Sitting next to Wayne.

He whispered against her cheek. "I will always love you." The intensity of his words rumbled in the pit of her belly.

She looked away and reached for her seatbelt. "Turbulence."

He laughed softly. "That wasn't turbulence, Cree Ann. That was you. Loving me back."

Cree couldn't take any more. "I need to go to the restroom."

He stood to let her out, running a hand down her arm as she stood. He held on to her hand as she walked away and she could feel his eyes on her the whole way down the aisle.

"Do Jesus." She fanned herself. Four more hours to go.

When she got back to her seat, he looked even drowsier.

"You should sleep. Okay?"

He nodded. He covered their top halves with his blanket and their bottom halves with hers. He pulled her right up against his body and grabbed her knee like he owned it. Within seconds, he was breathing deeply.

Cree hoped Wayne didn't wake up. Seeing them like that might jeopardize her check and as much as she was enjoying being with David, she wasn't trying to lose her money. She leaned against David's shoulder and tried to go to sleep. But she couldn't. Her mind was racing with possibilities.

Was God this kind to her? That she could get out of debt, fall back in love with the man of her dreams, all on the way to her sister's wedding in Kenya? The real question was, could she actually open her heart to let it happen?

Her sisters always teased her about being a serial dater but the truth was, any time she felt anything for any man, she also felt the need to run. Not that it happened often. Most of the men she met were busters – not worth her time except for the meal they were buying. But there might have been like three she had met over the last ten years that could have possibly been a possibility. She'd shut her heart down and run at the first hint of any feeling beyond attraction.

She never wanted to give her heart away like she had given it to Wayne. To give that much of herself – her whole heart – and to have it mean so little to him – she swore she'd never go through anything like that again.

She lifted her head off of David's shoulder. Sleep wasn't coming. She put her headphones back on and started scrolling through the movies. She paused when she saw Sanaa Lathan's face. She was her favorite actress. It was about some love triangle between Sanaa, Morris Chestnut, and Boris Kodjoe. Mmmmm...serious eye candy. Cree remembered seeing the movie advertised, but had never gotten to go see it. Unlike her, but she had been busy trying to get a business off the ground. She wasn't even sure what it was about.

She pushed play, snuggled into David's side like he was hers and started watching the movie.

Halfway in, her stomach started churning. Sanaa Lathan was playing the role of a carefree artist who falls in love with a political activist/preacher. In public, he's perfect and moral, charismatic and dynamic. But behind closed doors, he's emotionally abusive and a sex addict. He lived a double life, preaching abstinence but wanting sex every single day. She finally gets the strength the break away from the relationship and meets Mr. Perfect – Morris Chestnut. They fall in love fast and start a relationship. Six weeks in, she finds out she's pregnant with Mr. Preacher's baby. She and Mr. Perfect haven't had sex because – well, he's perfect. She can't stand the thought of having Mr. Preacher's baby and doesn't want to lose Mr. Perfect, so against everything in her, she has an abortion.

While Cree watched the clinic scene unfold, it was like all the air had been sucked out of the plane. Was she having some *Twilight Zone*, parallel universe experience? Had the writer peeked into her life and decided it made a fine story to put on the big screen? She looked from left to right. Both men were sleeping soundly and didn't see the tears falling down her cheeks.

Everything in her wanted to turn off the movie and not remember. Not remember what happened after Wayne left her. The first few mornings after she moved back in with her old roommate, when she started vomiting. And feeling tired. For weeks, she pretended nothing was happening. But she had missed her like-clockwork period, so she knew.

After a few weeks of denial and begging God, she felt like she was left with no choice. Somehow, Cree Ann Jordan, daughter of Evelyn and Nathaniel Jordan, raised in a Christian home with plenty of love and good values – taught to believe in the beauty of family above else – found herself sitting in an abortion clinic. Wondering how she got there.

She never told a soul. How could she? Who could she tell? Certainly not anyone in the Jordan family. Not even her grandmother who was her heart and made her feel as if she could do no wrong.

It was a secret she would take to her grave.

Cree couldn't help but fasten her eyes back on the movie. In spite of the piercing pain arrowing through her heart, she couldn't stop watching.

Even though Sanaa had the abortion so she could stay with Mr. Perfect, she went through a bad depression afterwards. She pushed him away. She never told Mr. Preacher about the baby. She never told Mr. Perfect why she couldn't be with him. And then she started dating man after man, having sex with complete strangers and losing herself. There were other pregnancies and other abortions. She started using drugs and ended up in rehab.

All Cree could say was thank God for Jesus. She could understand the emotions the actress was so perfectly portraying. She had felt them herself. She could have ended up on drugs with that pain she had gone through. But God…

In rehab, there's this scene with Sanaa and a therapist. The therapist is trying to figure out how a college-educated, beautiful, successful young woman became a sex and drug addict. She keeps asking all these probing questions and Sanaa just sits there in her chair, looking dead, eyes glazed over.

The therapist gets up in her face and says, "Tell me what happened to you? What did this to you? When I look past the deadness in your eyes, I can see you. This is not you. You're beautiful.

You're strong. You're artistic, creative. You're amazing. Who did this to you?"

And then she said the line that cut Cree's breath off. "You can keep these secrets if you want to, but I promise you, they'll kill you. You plan to take these secrets to your grave, but guess what? The secrets are going to take you to your grave."

The words ricocheted through Cree's brain, echoing into her soul. *You plan to take these secrets to your grave, but the secrets are going take you to your grave.*

Sobs hitched in her throat. She prayed she wouldn't wake Wayne or David. She looked up at the screen and saw Sanaa was doing the same thing. Except she had a full-fledged, ugly cry going on. She screamed and cried and screamed and cried. The therapist held her and said, "Set yourself free. You have to let it out so you can set yourself free."

Cree kept crying, but there was no therapist to hold her and rock her. Only her version of Mr. Preacher and Mr. Perfect flanking her on each side. There was a flood running from her eyes and nose down her face. She took her portion of the blanket and kept wiping her face, but the tears and snot kept coming.

Sanaa confesses everything to the therapist, and true to Hollywood style, her face all of a sudden starts shining and her eyes are bright. After several therapy sessions, she checks out of rehab, ready to take over the world again.

The next scene did Cree in. The therapist persuaded her that the only way to get rid of the guilt was to confess to Mr. Preacher that she had aborted his baby. The guilt had been eating her up for years and it was the reason she'd never been able to have a relationship again.

When Sanaa pulled up to Mr. Preacher's megachurch and knocked on his office door to confess the abortion, Cree couldn't take it anymore. She had to get up and away. She wished she had a parachute and could jump out of this plane that was choking the life out of her. The movie, the men, the thoughts, the emotions, her past. But jumping out of the plane wouldn't fix it. All of her stuff would go right out of the plane with her.

She tried to gently untangle herself from David's arms and from the blanket, but when she pulled his arm from around her waist, he woke up.

She tried to hide her face. "Let me out. I need to go to the restroom."

A sleepy smile crossed his face like he was happy to wake up with her in his arms. But then his eyes focused and she knew he saw. "Cree Ann...what's wrong? What happened?"

"Nothing. I need to get to the restroom. Please, let me out."

He didn't move and reached out to touch her face. She jerked away from him. "Please! MOVE."

He looked completely confused, but stood to let her out. "Cree Ann…"

She shut him down with a "talk to the hand gesture" and halfway ran down the aisle to the restroom. When she locked herself inside the cramped space, she was finally alone. She sat on top of the toilet seat and cried from the deepest place in her soul, letting out ten years worth of tears.

Chapter 8

What had just happened? What did he miss? One minute, he and Cree were talking like old times. And then that kiss and the closeness. He had fallen asleep with her in his arms, inhaling her scent and then next thing he knew, her face was covered in tears.

He looked over at Wayne. What had that fool done? He had promised Cree he'd behave, but if Wayne had upset her, he planned to kill him. But he couldn't imagine that it was Wayne. He was still sleeping.

David looked at the headphones Cree had shoved into his hands before she left. His eyes trailed up to the movie screen. He saw that fine actress, Sanaa Lathan, on the screen crying in Morris Chestnut's arms.

Was that what Cree was crying about? A movie? He knew she was an artist and all sensitive and stuff, but he had never known her to cry through a movie. And he had suffered through plenty a chick flick with her back in the day.

He thought about going after her, but decided to give her space. How far could she go? They were on a plane after all. She'd eventually come back to her seat and he'd find out what was going on.

He hoped he hadn't rushed her with his persistence, but being with her felt so natural. Her talking. Her in his arms. In ten years, he had never stopped loving her. In fact, after years of blah blah relationships that never went anywhere, he knew he loved her more now than he ever had. Well, one had gone pretty far. Almost to the point of marriage. He pushed Kara out of his mind. No sense going there.

The last time he had seen Cree cry like that was the last time he had seen her. When she broke up with him. To this day, he didn't know what that was about. She had left his apartment to go break up with Wayne. He wasn't the kind of guy that wanted to be with another man's woman and she didn't feel comfortable two-timing Wayne. But it was like they couldn't get enough of each other. They promised to stop seeing each other until she figured things out with Wayne but they kept ending up together. They were inseparable. They just needed to get Wayne from between them.

Cree stayed gone forever. He finally couldn't wait anymore and decided to go check on her. When he got back to the restroom area, the stewardess that had been keeping Cree's chocolate supply abundant was standing outside the door. She gave him a half smile.

"She's fine. I got her. She'll be back in a minute." She motioned with her hand for him to go back to his seat. He heard the microwave ding and the stewardess removed two hot towels like they gave the people in first class. She knocked on the door and it opened. She passed the towels inside and closed the door again.

When she saw him still standing there, she pursed her lips. "I told you I got her. Don't no woman want her man to see her crying and tore up. In fact, bring me her make-up bag. Just bring me her whole purse. Go on, now." She waved him down the aisle with both hands.

He went back to their seat and lifted the blankets to find Cree's purse. Her whole half of the blanket was saturated and soggy. What was she really crying about? He stared at the movie. Morris Chestnut and Sanaa Lathan were getting married on the beach. He pushed the touch screen and the title flashed. He hadn't dated anyone in the last year so there was absolutely no reason for him to have watched the chick flick. He'd Google it later to figure out what had messed Cree up so bad.

He turned around to head back down the aisle to take Cree's purse, but the stewardess was standing right behind him. He almost bumped into her.

She pursed her lips again, held out her hand like he was a disobedient child. "Give me the bag." She rolled her eyes.

"I didn't do it. It wasn't me." Why was he defending himself to a stranger?

She smiled. "I know. She's just going through some stuff."

"What did she say?" It was unlike Cree to spill her guts to a stranger. But then again, it was unlike her to saturate a blanket with tears. "What's wrong?"

The stewardess shrugged. "I don't know. She didn't say anything. I just know us. I can tell she loves you and she's going to be fine. Now sit down. She'll be back, looking pretty as ever real soon." She patted him on the shoulder reassuringly and he sat down.

She loves you and she's going to be fine. He was going to have to hold on to that.

True to the stewardess' word, Cree came back fifteen minutes later looking like nothing ever happened. The swollen, bloodshot eyes were gone, her make-up was perfect and he couldn't even tell she had been crying. What had the stewardess done? Some black girl magic for sure.

He stood to let her back in her seat and sat down next to her. He wasn't sure what to do. He wished he had asked the stewardess since she seemed to know so much.

"Hey?" he said it almost like a question.

"Hey." Cree let out a deep breath. Even though her face looked perfect, he could tell her heart wasn't.

"You okay?" He reached out for her hand,

but she drew away from him.

She let out a deep breath. "Please, David. I…"

He looked into her eyes. When they threatened to fill with tears again, he decided it was best to leave her alone. He had gotten rid of the soaked blanket so he gave her his. He wrapped the cord around her headphones and pushed them into her purse. He fluffed her pillow behind her. "We have less than two hours before they start serving breakfast. You should try to sleep. Okay?"

She nodded and looked into his eyes for about three seconds before she dropped her head. "Thanks," she mumbled.

He placed the armrest back between them, sensing that for whatever reason – whatever she had seen in that movie that sent her off an emotional cliff – she wanted her distance. She sat there for a second, lifted the armrest and snuggled into his side, pulling the blanket over her.

He smiled. He guessed the stewardess was right again. He repeated the words to himself like a mantra. *She loves me and she's going be fine. She loves me and she's going to be fine.*

He hoped he was Morris Chestnut to her Sanaa Lathan and that they would end up with their happily ever after.

***

By the time they walked off the plane and

into Charles de Gaulle airport in Paris, Cree had gotten her two hours of sleep. She slept like a rock in his side. She slept through breakfast. He hadn't wanted to wake her so he refused breakfast as well and sat still so she could sleep. Wayne had slept, too.

Both of them woke up when the plane touched down. Wayne had scowled when he woke first to see Cree cuddled up against him. It took everything within David not to smirk a triumphant smirk. Instead, he jostled Cree to wake her up so they could get ready to deplane.

He planned to buy her breakfast during their three-hour layover. He wished they had a longer layover so he could take her out to see Paris. He had made a trip to Paris a few years back and knew she would appreciate the museums and architecture of the city. If things turned out the way he planned, maybe he'd bring her back on another trip.

Before breakfast, his first plan was to go to the ticket counter to get their seats changed so they could sit together again. He had another eight-hour flight to seal the deal with her. If the flight wasn't sold out, maybe he would buy the third seat in their row so there was no chance of Wayne crashing their party again.

They walked to the gate together, him pulling her carry-on. He wasn't sure what happened to Wayne. He was probably mad and pouting somewhere. When they got to the gate, David squinted at the sign.

Air France 8002 operated by Kenya Airways
9:12 am – Cancelled

He turned around just in time to see shock register on Cree's face.

"Cree Ann, it's okay. Let me find out what's going on and figure out what to do. We'll get you to Brooke's wedding." He led her to a seat at the gate and went up to the counter to talk to the attendant.

It didn't take long to find out that the flight was cancelled and the next flight out was scheduled for the same time the next day – 9:12 am. There were no other flights headed to Kenya and there was nothing they could do about it. They had been assigned a hotel room in the Sheraton there at the airport, were to be issued food vouchers and that was that. No other options. He wasn't one to argue, especially when there was obviously no point.

Cree had been listening the whole time. He thought she would throw a fit and try to argue like she had in Atlanta, but either she realized there was no hope or whatever had happened on the plane had taken the fire out of her. He hoped it wasn't the latter.

He knew it was wrong, but he was secretly glad for a whole additional 24 hours with her. He'd get to take her to see Paris after all. His mind started ticking through all the places he knew the artist in her would love. When he saw the disappointment in her eyes, he pushed his joy to the side.

"Sorry."

Cree shrugged. "It's okay. There's nothing that can be done. This whole trip is turning into a disaster."

He tried not to be upset about the fact that she considered their meeting again a disaster but it felt like a kick in the gut.

She must have sensed his reaction because she said, "I mean, not a total disaster. I'm sorry. I just want to get to Brooke." She sighed. "I'm her maid of honor and I'm not there to do anything. Arielle had to help her pick out her dress. Today, we were supposed to finalize the menu and me and Arielle were supposed to get our dresses. And then we were supposed to have the bridal shower this evening. By the time I get there, I'll have only two days left before she gets married and isn't my sister first anymore. She'll be Marcus' wife first and then my sister. I wanted a little more time before I lose her."

"You're not losing her. But I know what you mean." He grabbed her carry-on and looked up for the airport exit signs that would lead them to the hotel. "Come on. Let's get some breakfast and go see Paris."

She frowned. "I just want to sleep."

"Are you kidding me? We have a free 24 hours in Paris and you want to sleep? No way. You're not missing this opportunity."

"I'm exhausted."

"You're telling me you don't want to go see the Louvre? You don't want to see the Mona Lisa? And Notre Dame? And the Eiffel tower? Come on, Cree Ann. The artist in you will never forgive yourself. When will you get back here again?"

He could tell he had gotten to her when a faraway look entered her eyes. Then she squinted. "Wait. What you know about Paris? You've been here before?"

"Yes, ma'am. And I'm offering my services as your personal tour guide for the day. I'll take you everywhere. It'll be the best day ever."

Her face clouded over. "I can't afford a day in Paris. I'm a starving artist with a new business. I can hardly afford a cup of coffee, let alone a tour of the city. I'll be fine in my hotel room. It'll give me a chance to sleep before I get to my maid of honor duties."

He leaned close to her. "If you let me, I'll take care of everything. The whole day. " He tried to keep the beg out of his voice but he couldn't. There was no way he was going to let this chance slip away.

She stared at him for a second. She tried not

to, but her eyes trailed to his clothes and his old leather bag. Did she think he was broke? Probably so. He had said he was a nomad backpacking around the country and she had obviously come to the conclusion that he was a broke nomad.

He had to laugh. "Cree Ann, I'm taking you out today and I'm not taking no for an answer."

She smiled shyly. It did him in when she did that. Brash, brazen Cree was shy, quiet and blushing in his presence. "Okay. But I don't have any clothes to wear."

His eyes widened and he held up her heavy carry-on bag. "What's in here?" he asked incredulously.

Cree bit her lip. "Shoes and make-up. And underwear. But no clothes."

David laughed. "Some things never change." He eyed her up and down. "You look like you're still a size 6, right?"

Her eyes widened.

"You'd be surprised how much I remember about you, Cree Ann..." He loved saying her name long and slow. He could tell she liked it, too.

A frown crossed her face. David turned to see Wayne approaching. He looked back at Cree and it was as if a dark cloud drifted over her head. Whatever had happened last night had everything to do with Wayne. Something must have happened in the movie that reminded her about something between the two of them.

"What's going on?" Wayne stared past them at the gate. "Cancelled? Seriously?"

"They've booked hotel rooms for us and the rest of the team. We'll spend the night in Paris and leave in the morning," David said. "Have you seen Jim? We'll need to let him know so he can notify our host in Kenya that we're losing a day of the trip."

"They're behind us. Should be here soon." Wayne looked at him and then at Cree.

David said, "I'm getting Cree to the hotel. She had a rough night on the plane."

Wayne moved over in front of Cree. "Don't forget about our breakfast."

Cree visibly flinched. "Wayne, I don't think I can. Can it wait until we get back to the U.S.?"

He shrugged. "Your choice. If you want to let things go, we can."

David could see the anger surging through Cree's body. "Fine," she said through tight lips. "Let me sleep for a couple of hours. I'll find your room number and call you and we can meet in the hotel lobby."

"Hotel lobby? Baby, we're in Paris. Let me take you out somewhere nice. This is the City of Love."

Cree let out a deep breath. "Wayne, please. I'm not in that kind of mood. We can experience the city of love in the hotel lobby or not at all. I'll call you when I wake up." She looked up at David and walked toward the exit.

David wanted to punch the "I got the girl – again" smirk off Wayne's face. He followed Cree. "What was that about? I thought you were spending the day with me?"

She let out a deep breath and he was afraid the tears would start to fall again. He didn't want to push her, but didn't want to lose her either. "Cree?"

She hesitated. "I have to talk to him. We have…unfinished business."

"What unfinished business could you possibly have with him?" He could see she was really struggling with whatever was going on. "Cree, you've spent a few hours with Wayne and you're already sad. He's already sucked the joy out of you. Again. Some things never change."

Cree's pace quickened and David increased his stride to keep up with her.

"You said you haven't seen him in years, so what kind of hold does he have over you?"

"He doesn't have a hold. We just have…history."

"History that takes the light out of your eyes?"

"It's not about Wayne."

"Then tell me. What is it?"

Cree's kept walking and he could tell she

was trying to keep her emotions under control.

He reached for her arm and stopped her. "Cree Ann, we're in Paris. I haven't seen you in years. You don't have to ever see me again if you don't want to, so unload whatever it is. Get it off your chest, so you can move on."

"It's not that easy. I..."

"What is it? Please, let me help you. It's not good to hold it in. Holding stuff in will only make you sad. It can kill you."

The tears started falling. "David, please just leave me alone." Cree took her carry-on from his hand and ran toward the escalator leading from the terminal straight into the hotel.

What hold did Wayne have on her? It was like she was a crack addict and Wayne was her pusher. Just like back then, he made her miserable and yet she kept going back. What was it? If he could figure it out, maybe he could set her free. But was it worth it? Was he willing to risk his heart again, fighting a fool that wasn't worth his or Cree's time? He shook his head. No, she had to see it for herself.

He knew she had to have felt the attraction between them on the plane. It was like time hadn't stolen ten years from them. Yesteryear felt like yesterday when the two of them were together.

David caught up with her at the hotel lobby check-in desk. He didn't know what to say. He felt her slipping away from him again and he didn't know whether he should just let it happen or fight for her.

He stood silently while she checked in and got her room key. Before she left for her room, he said, "I wish you wouldn't have that breakfast with him."

She looked up at him. "I told you. This isn't about Wayne. This is about me making peace with my past." She walked off toward the elevator.

The stewardess' words came back to him. *She loves you and she's going to be fine.* He decided that he wasn't going to give her up again without giving it his best fight.

Chapter 9

Cree let the hotel door close behind her. She dropped both bags and fell across the bed in a heap of tears. She didn't think she had any left from the plane but after a few minutes, she had soaked the thick duvet cover on the bed.

She couldn't stop thinking about that day. When she had killed her baby. Wayne's baby that he didn't know anything about. He was wrong for dumping her, but it didn't give her the right to kill his child without him even knowing.

She remembered the six months of depression that started the moment she left that clinic. She had killed a child. She had killed a baby. Her baby. She felt like a murderer. The guilt came back as strong as it had been back then. She made her mind go blank and her heart go numb as she'd had to just to survive ten years ago.

She took in some deep breaths and tried to calm down. She had to get herself together. In 24 hours, she had to become the best maid of honor her sister could ever ask for. Even though she had missed some major duties she was responsible for, she still needed to be there for Brooke. And she couldn't do that if she was all in her feelings.

Brooke. She had to tell her she was delayed another day. She went to the bathroom and splashed her face with cold water. Then she did the stewardess' trick. She ran the water hot and saturated a washcloth. She put the washcloth as hot as she could stand against her eyes a few times. Then she applied a freezing cold washcloth. Just like magic, the swelling and redness went away.

Who was she fooling? Brooke would take one look at her and know she'd been crying. She'd want to know what happened. This was Brooke's special time and she didn't want to ruin it with her drama. Maybe she'd Facetime one of her brothers and tell them to let Brooke know about the flight cancellation. No, that would only alert Brooke all the more that something was wrong.

She decided to try her sister, Arielle. She returned to the bedroom and pulled her phone out of her bag. When she touched Arielle's name on the screen and the camera put her face on the screen, she cringed and immediately hung up. She went back to the bathroom and put on some eye makeup and light lipstick. Enough to make her look a little better, but not enough to make it look like she was trying.

She dialed Arielle again. It rang about five times without an answer. She wasn't sure of the time difference between Paris and Kenya, but she knew it had to be early since her phone said it was 7 a.m. There was no way Arielle was awake yet. She hung up and dialed Brooke.

Brooke, ever the early bird, picked up on the second ring. "Creesie! You've landed in Paris. You're halfway here! We've already got a driver ready to come get you this afternoon."

The excitement on her face and joy in her voice did Cree in. She started to cry.

"Cree, what in the world? What's wrong with you?"

"My flight is cancelled. I won't get there until tomorrow afternoon."

"Oh, honey, it's okay. Stop crying."

"I'm missing everything. What are you guys doing today? Where is everybody? How was the dinner last night?" Cree started crying harder. "I'm missing all the fun."

"Cree, seriously? What's wrong with you?"

This was exactly what she had planned not to do. She quickly wiped her face and sucked up her snot. "Nothing. I couldn't sleep on the plane. I'm tired. And I'm disappointed that I'm letting you down by not being there."

"Yeah, uh huh. What's really going on?"

"Nothing. If I could sprout wings to get there I would. This is all about your special day. I never should have gone to that conference. I'm sorry, girl."

Cree heard a cranky voice behind Brooke. "Why y'all heifers always got to be waking me up all early in the morning?" Cree could hear a loud yawn. "What is all that blabbering and crying about?"

Brooke swung the camera around for Cree to see Arielle's grumpy morning face.

"Good morning, Sunshine," Cree sang out. Just seeing her sisters made her feel a little better.

Arielle wiped the sleep out of her eyes and focused on Cree on the screen. "Heifer, what's wrong with you? Why your face looking all jacked up like that? And why are you in a hotel room? What's going on?"

Cree told them about all the problems with the flight, conveniently leaving out the whole Wayne and David catastrophe.

"And…" they both demanded when she finished.

"And what?"

"Cree, stop playing. We know you. Something more than a cancelled flight got your face looking all crazy," Brooke said, and then the lightbulb came on. Cree could see it in her expression. "Wait a minute. Does this have anything to do with you seeing Wayne at the airport? Did he say something to you?"

"Wayne?" Arielle interrupted. "Dude from back in the day? You saw Wayne in Atlanta?" Arielle turned to Brooke. "Why didn't you tell me?"

"I didn't think it was that big of a deal, but apparently it was." Brooke turned from Arielle back to Cree. They both stared at the screen. "What happened? Spill it."

"Brooke, no. This week is about you and your wedding. You're marrying your prince. You don't need to hear about my drama with my frog."

"So there was drama with Wayne. What happened?" Arielle had that "I'ma snatch off my earrings and fight" look in her eyes.

"Girl, please. Can we focus on Brooke? Please?" She knew her sisters well enough to know they wouldn't let it go. "And besides I need to get some sleep. I was up all night."

"You were up all night? The girl that can sleep through anything? Okay, this is really serious. Start talking or we're catching a plane to Paris." Arielle folded her arms and Brooke nodded her agreement.

What could she even tell them? They didn't know much about her history with Wayne, except that he broke her heart. He had come to their family Thanksgiving dinner once, but that was when things were good. No one in her family knew that the student loans she had racked up while her parents were paying her tuition and fees were because of Wayne. They just chalked it up to crazy, carefree, indulgent Cree. She was crazy and carefree, but not $30,000 worth of either.

She had mentioned David briefly in a late night conversation over Twix bars and ice cream with her sisters. They both swore he was the one that got away and their urging was what persuaded Cree to Google David and try to find him a few years back. When the search came up empty, they had all been disappointed, but that was the end of that.

"Creesie! Come back. This is not the time to fly off into your daydream world. We need to know what's going on."

She stared into both of her sisters' eagerly awaiting faces. "Ugh. Can't I tell you when I get there? This conversation calls for Twix and ice cream. They got that in Kenya?"

Brooke laughed. "They got anything here you could think of or want. Wait until you see the resort. It's amazing. This is such a beautiful country."

Arielle chimed in. "You wouldn't believe all the stuff we've seen. Just driving on the highway, we've seen zebras and antelopes and here at the resort, there's these cute little monkeys…"

A little joy bubbled in her heart. Crisis averted. At least momentarily. Her sisters chatted on for a while about the beauty of Kenya, especially about the trip from Nairobi to the resort where the wedding would take place. She let their chatter take her away from her problems.

"Okay, get some sleep then." Brooke's voice interrupted her thoughts. She realized she'd been listening to them, but somehow the talk about the beauty of Kenya led her mind to drift to David and the brief conversation he'd shared about his own excitement about seeing the country. Brooke continued. "There's plenty to do when you get here and plenty to see. We want you as rested as possible."

Arielle added, "Forget about Wayne. You bumping into him was a dumb coincidence. You don't ever have to see him again in this life or the next."

Cree bit her lip. There was no way she was telling her sisters she was about to meet him for breakfast. They ended the call. She hopped up from the bed and decided to take a shower before she tried to sleep. While in the shower, she washed out her blouse and hung it to dry. Her jeans were fine and she had plenty of underwear and more than enough pairs of shoes.

She dried off and wrapped the soft, thick hotel robe around herself and crawled into the bed. She tried to sleep for about an hour but she couldn't stop thinking about that stupid movie. Was what the therapist said true? Would her secrets take her to an early grave? It wasn't like she was the girl in the movie – having serial abortions and using drugs.

The worst that she'd done was have serial boyfriends. Her mind scrolled back through all the men she had dated over the years. She thought hard and realized she had never gotten past the two-month mark with any of them. She frowned.

Wait, was that really true?

She sat up in bed, going through their faces and the few names she remembered. She hadn't been serious about a man since Wayne. And David.

The thought smacked her in the middle of her chest and made her sadder than seeing Wayne and watching that stupid movie. As tough as she tried to be, she really did want to get married one day. And even though everybody thought she was wild and irresponsible, she wanted to have babies. At least two. She wanted a beautiful family. A good husband and two, pretty babies. Or three. She was a Jordan after all and family was everything. She didn't want to grow old alone.

And now that Brooke was getting married, everybody was going to be looking at her. All her brothers were married except Gage and he'd just gotten engaged to Raine. Cade was newly divorced from his witch of a wife, Savant, so nobody would bother him for a while. Arielle was too stubborn and independent for her mother and grandmother to be throwing hints about marriage and children. That left her. As soon as Brooke was married off, all eyes in the Jordan family would be turned to her. "So when you going to get married, Cree?" She groaned just thinking about it.

Maybe she wasn't sexing and having

abortions and using drugs, but she seemed to be incapable of having a long-term relationship. And she couldn't really say she hadn't met anybody in all this time that was marriage material. She hadn't given anyone that much of a chance. After Wayne, she had sworn she would never love that hard and give away that much again. And she'd stayed true to her word. But where had it gotten her?

Alone, crying under the covers in Paris.

Her phone rang with her Facetime ringtone. She saw Brooke's name. She should have known Brooke wouldn't let it go. She answered the call.

"What?" she snapped. "I told you heifers I needed to sleep and we would talk when I got there."

"How I use this thing?"

The voice coming through the speaker wasn't Brooke's.

"Just talk Grandma," Brooke said. "Look, see Cree's face. She can see your face, too."

Cree's heart caught in her chest. They had pulled out the big guns on her. Her sisters didn't play fair at all. "Good morning, Grandma."

"Hey Creebaby. How's my girl doing?"

Warmth filled Cree's chest. Her grandmother's face only had a few, fine wrinkles and age spots and she only had a light sprinkling of grey hair at her temples. No one would believe she was seventy-five.

"Fine, grandma. I'm fine."

"Why you gon' lie to your grandma? What I do to you?"

"Grandma, I'm fine. I was on a plane all night and didn't sleep. If my sisters would let me rest, I would be okay. I'll be all fresh and ready to see you guys by tomorrow afternoon."

"Babygirl, you can save that for somebody that don't know you. This is your grandmother you talking too. Look at your face. Who done made my baby cry? It's a whole lot of trees in this Kenya. I can go pick a switch and take care of whoever needs taking care of."

Cree laughed and a stray tear eased down her face. She loved her grandmother with all her heart. Her voice sounded like fresh out of the oven chocolate chip cookies and Thanksgiving sweet potato pie. Her smile felt like a warm hug on a sad day and her hugs felt like being swallowed up in a big ol' bucket of love.

"Grandma, there ain't nobody you need to take a switch to for me." Cree laughed, though, imagining Grandma Jordan's taking a switch to Wayne's behind. If she knew the whole story, she'd beat him real good. Cree laughed again just thinking about Grandma running after Wayne, swatting him with a switch and telling him about himself.

"There's my babygirl's smile. That's what I'm talking 'bout. Now what's wrong wit' you?

Who made you cry and why you let 'em do it?"

"Grandma, just like I told my sisters, it's not anything to talk about over the phone. I promise I'll tell you guys when I get there."

"Ummmhmmm…" Then Grandma Jordan did what she always did. She stared at her face real hard. Cree wanted to turn the camera away from herself but it would only make her grandmother fuss. She stared at her for a full minute and then finally spoke.

"Creebaby, I'ma tell you like I always tell you. Everything happens for a reason and God is always in control." She stared at her for another minute. Cree didn't know how, but Grandma always *knew.* Even when Cree didn't tell her what was going on, her grandmother knew exactly what to say.

"Whatever happened to you yesterday is God's doing. You been carrying around some stuff for too long and He's ready to set you free. But you gotta let him. If you hold onto it, it'll keep eating you up and keep you from getting the life you want." Grandma paused to take a breath and then released it on a winded sigh. "If you let it go…babygirl, you'll be free and so happy. Let it go. You hear me? Let it go."

Cree was crying again.

"You're my strong, brave beautiful girl. It's time for you to be free. I want you happy and God wants you happy. You hear me?"

Cree nodded. She was too choked with tears to speak.

"Okay, then. I'll see you when you get here. I don't know what it is, but you do what you got to do. You hear?"

"Yes, ma'am."

"Grandma loves you, Creebaby."

Cree choked out, "I love you too, Grandma."

"Brookie, come here. How you hang this thing up?"

The screen went black.

Cree let out a deep breath. She got up off the bed and washed her face. She was ready to do what she had to do to set herself free.

Chapter 10

Cree called the front desk and asked to be connected to Wayne's room. Within seconds the phone was ringing.

"Hello?" His voice was full of sleep. How could he still be tired after sleeping the whole night on the plane?

"Wayne, it's Cree."

"Good morning, baby. You ready for our breakfast? I found out that there's a nice café bakery a few train stops from here. We can –"

"Meet me in the hotel lobby restaurant in half an hour."

"Come on baby, don't be like that. Let me take you out."

Cree rolled her eyes. "Wayne, it's there or not at all."

"Okay then. Maybe we shouldn't meet at all. I was trying to make things right and pay off my debt, but you act like – "

"Like I said on the plane, if you want to pay back the money, pay it. But you're not going to hold it over my head to try to restart something that died years ago. Let me know whether I should be downstairs in half an hour."

"Ok, baby. I'll be there." He knew her well enough to know that's all he was getting.

"And if you call me baby one more time, I *will* punch you in the throat. I've been wanting to try that move on somebody for a while now and you'd be the perfect candidate."

He let out a deep breath. "Cree, you haven't changed at all. Still got all that mouth."

"Yep. Act like you know." She hung up the phone.

She pulled on her jeans and then walked into the bathroom to put on her shirt. It was wringing wet. She had forgotten she had washed it. She sucked her teeth and looked around. She didn't have another thing to put on and she knew anything from the hotel lobby boutique was going to be super, ridiculous expensive.

She pulled the blow dryer off its perch on the bathroom wall and started blowing the shirt. She was going to have to call Wayne back and tell him it was going to be an hour instead. Just as she was about to pick up the phone, there was a knock at the door.

He better not have come to her room. She put her eye up to the little hole in the door. It was a person in a Sheraton uniform. "Yes?"

"You have a delivery from the boutique downstairs."

Cree frowned, covered her chest with a towel and opened the door. The young guy with a thick French accent handed her a bag. She said thanks and shut the door. She hoped he wasn't expecting a tip or anything. She ripped the note off the bag. Ten years later, she still remembered David's handwriting.

For our day in Paris. I'm sure you have shoes to match. Call me after breakfast. ~David

She opened the bag and pulled out a dress made of the most beautiful, silky fabric she had ever felt. It was a burnt orange, wrap dress that would accent her waist and then flare and end right above the knee. He had remembered how much she loved the color, how it brought out her hair. The tag had been removed, but she knew the dress had to cost a fortune. She shopped. She knew her textiles.

Cree walked across the room to the full length mirror in the corner and held the dress against her body. She felt her eyes moisten again, but thankfully it was from happiness instead of sadness. She smiled. She wasn't going to cry about this.

But where did a nomad backpacker get that kind of money? She had spent her time with David doing all the talking but today, she wanted to hear from him. What was his real story?

She quickly pulled off her jeans and tried on the dress. It fit her perfectly and she looked better than gorgeous. The dress made her feel supersexy.

She spun around, admiring herself until she'd had her fill – until all her Cree Jordan confidence was back. "Oh David, you trying to get 'chose'."

She touched up her make-up, fluffed up her curls and blew herself a kiss in the mirror. She didn't plan to have a long breakfast with Wayne. She just wanted to deliver her soul and then go spend the day in the City of Love with the man that bought her this dress. She was spending the day with a man she hadn't had to manipulate or guilt into opening his wallet. That was magic in and of itself.

***

By the time the elevator made its way to the lobby, some of her confidence and most of her courage had waned. Nervousness settled into her stomach. What was she supposed to say? "I aborted your child ten years ago. I'm sorry?" Who does that? Who says that to a minister? Even a bootleg minister like Wayne had to have some convictions about abortion.

Wayne was sitting at the table in his now rumpled, expensive suit he had worn on the plane. He didn't have a carry-on bag, just an expensive brief case, so she knew he didn't have a change of clothes. She was surprised he hadn't bought something flashy to wear at the boutique.

His eyes bugged out of his head when she

walked up to the table. She knew it wasn't necessary, but she stood there for a minute, letting him look her up and down, admiring her "Cree-ness." When she was satisfied that she had given him enough, she sat down across from him.

"Wayne."

"Cree. Wow…you look…amazing."

"Thanks." She gathered her courage and tried to find her words.

He kept grinning and talking. "I can't believe I'm seeing you after all these years. And you look so good. This was meant to be. I was actually thinking about you the other day and – "

"I have something to tell you," Cree's blurted out. "I have something to say and if I don't say it right now I may never do it."

Wayne stretched his arm across the table and covered her hand. "What is it, baby?"

Baby…She looked at his throat, resisting the overwhelming urge to throw a jab at his Adam's Apple. And now she realized why it bothered her so much for him to call her that. It wasn't just because he had no right to utter a term of endearment. It was the choice of the word 'baby' that was subconsciously as wicked as any four-letter word she'd ever heard.

Cree took a deep breath and held it as she spit the words, "I had an abortion in college."

He looked thoughtful for a second. It wasn't

the reaction she had expected at all. "When?"

"After we broke up. A few weeks after."

He was quiet for a good while. "I knew you had an abortion, Cree."

Cree jerked back from the table. "What do you mean you knew?"

"I knew is what I meant." His tone was so matter-of-fact that it was hard to process what he was saying.

"Why haven't you ever said anything?"

Wayne shook his head and reached for a sweaty water goblet in front of his place setting. "What's to say? You made a decision and I respected it." He took a sip.

"Oh my God. It never occurred to you that it was a hard decision? To try to go through it with me?"

"That would have been too much like cosigning to what you were doing."

"You let me go through that alone?"

"That wasn't something I could…do. Or be a part of."

"So, you were okay with me having the abortion as long as you didn't have to say so?"

"Cree, that was ten years ago. What does it matter now?" His phone buzzed. He put down the glass and picked it up.

She wanted to snatch it from him and drop it in his glass. "It matters that you knew, because all this time I've carried this. All by myself. And it's practically ruined my life."

He raised an eyebrow. "Okay, I'm here now. What do you need?" He looked down at his phone again and held up a finger before he typed something.

"What do I need?" She had to fight the urge to scream. "I need you to feel…something. To do something other than scroll through your Instagram."

"I'm on Twitter." He placed the phone down and returned his hand to hers. She snatched it back. "Do you feel better now that you've told me? Is that what's been holding you back, because baby, I want you to know, I forgive you. I understand how hard it must have been for you. I encourage you to pray for God's forgiveness."

"God's forgiveness?" Cree was so mad she could hardly see straight. *Religious hypocrite…*

"I've forgiven you for that. We belong together. I love you. I've always loved you. I've sown my wild oats and now I'm ready to commit to you."

Cree ignored him, still unable to believe the conversation unfolding between them. "You knew and you didn't say anything and you call that always loving me? You loved me but you let me carry that alone?"

"You weren't alone. You had your family."

"So, what I was supposed to go home pregnant and say, 'I need help having an abortion by someone who dumped me after I ran up $30K in debt for him?' Was I supposed to admit to my family that I had been stupid enough to take out student loans to pay all your bills and medical expenses when you ran out of money and your insurance wouldn't cover your cancer treatment? And that you dumped me as soon as your cancer was gone? Is that what I was supposed to tell my father?"

"Cree, I'm sorry. I was young. Remember, we both were and I'm sorry for the decisions I made back then."

Wayne was talking too fast. So fast that she wondered if he had rehearsed this script. She thought he was done hurting her, that he didn't have the power to do it anymore, but he did. The devil always had someone he could use. She bit her lip and let about a long sigh.

"Here I felt guilty all these years because I terminated that pregnancy. I did something I don't even believe in, something I was completely against. And I felt like I took something away from you. I killed your baby without you knowing. But you knew and you didn't even care. This is almost funny. That's how pathetic it is."

"Cree, I'm sorry."

"Yeah, Wayne. You really are." She stood

and walked away from the table. Her legs were shaky and her stomach was churning, but she managed to enter the lobby. But then stopped. She wasn't about to let him off that easy.

Cree marched back to the table and jammed herself into the seat across from him again.

He smiled that arrogant smile again like he thought she had come back for him.

In his dreams…

"Baby, I can make this right. We can make this right. We were young and foolish, but now we're older and wiser."

She pulled her phone out of her purse and started tapping the touch screen.

He laughed to himself. "Remember how I used to joke that I was going to have to get rich so you could do your little artsy stuff and be a kept wife? Well, it's happened. I got enough to take care of you, baby. You can do your little greeting cards and your little coloring books and whatever other art you want to do. I can take care of us. Buy you everything you want. We can have some children and be a family. I've done real well for myself."

"I'm glad to hear that you're rich and you want to take care of me." She turned the phone toward him. "This is my banking information. Since you got all this money, you need to pay me back. You can transfer the money directly into my account."

Wayne frowned. He looked shocked. Really? What did he expect?

"That's not what I meant. I meant us, together. Give me a chance." He put a hand over hers and she recoiled from his touch.

He continued, "I can't believe you don't remember…us. I know things went bad, but –"

"I remember *us* very well. You're the one with amnesia. I remember wiping your tail when you couldn't wipe it yourself. I remember feeding you when you couldn't eat. I remember holding you all night when you thought you were going to die. And I remember the night we were supposed to celebrate your cure – you remember that night? The night you told me you were in love with another woman. Remember?"

Wayne looked down at his hands.

Cree continued. "Most of all, I remember $30,000. I can't forget it because I'm still trying to pay most of it back." She shoved the phone towards him. "So as I said, here's my banking information. You owe me $30,000. Plus interest."

Wayne let out a deep breath and picked up his phone and started tapping buttons. "I can give you half now. The other half I'll give you on Saturday, after you let me be your date at Brooke's wedding."

Cree frowned. What in the world was his problem? Had he not heard a word she said? "What would make you think I would want you as my date at Brooke's wedding? Why do you want to come to her wedding so bad? Do you know what my family would do to you if they saw you? You don't remember my brothers?"

Wayne's eyes stretched wide. He obviously remembered the tall, muscular men of the Jordan family, and how protective they were of their sisters. "What did you tell your brothers?"

Cree rolled her eyes. "Nothing. I didn't have to tell them anything. But my whole family knows you're the one that broke my heart. And for my brothers, that's all they need to know."

Wayne swallowed hard. "Can't you just tell them things are fine? That you've forgiven me and things are okay?"

"Why would I do that? What is your deal, Wayne?" Cree's brain was in overdrive. At first she thought she might need to say what she was saying another way, but she knew Wayne was a manipulative user. He wanted something.

She slid her phone across the table. Her heart leaped into her throat when he accepted it. Her leg shook every so slightly under the table. Was he about to transfer $30,000?

He slid the phone back. She refreshed the screen. $15,000. She couldn't be disappointed. It was enough to pay off most of what was left of the loan.

He reached across the table for her hand. Something about $15,000 made her let him take it.

"Let me come to the wedding. Let me make things right. Give me another chance. It was the cancer that made me act like that."

"Couldn't have been. You're still a jerk. Too bad surgery, chemo, and radiation can't cure that." She pulled her hand away.

"Cree, I love you."

"You don't love me. You are not capable of loving anyone."

"I've changed."

"Good. Maybe you can be a better man for someone else."

Cree stood and walked away from the table.

"We'll talk more on the plane," he called after her.

She came back and leaned close to his face and hissed, "We're not flying together again. Don't change your seat. Don't come near me. I'm done with you."

"If you want the rest of your money, you're not." He shrugged and crossed his arms over his chest like he was a man holding all the right cards. "Like I said, I'll transfer the other $15,000 after the wedding on Saturday."

Cree walked away. $15,000 would have to be enough.

Chapter 11

David sat in the lobby, waiting for Cree to come out of the restaurant. He had peeked in through the glass windows a few times, monitoring the conversation between her and Wayne. It didn't take him long to realize he had nothing to worry about. At one point it looked like she would rip Wayne's head off.

When she came out, he could tell she was furious, but something about her had changed. She didn't look sad and helpless any more. She looked like her old self again, large and in charge.

She was angry. She didn't see him when she stormed by. He let out a low whistle. She turned. She marched back toward him, nostrils flaring and eyes flashing.

"Wow..." he said under his breath. The mannequin had done nothing for the dress. Cree looked amazing. "You okay?"

"No...yes...no...arghhhh." She let out a low growl.

"Down, Tiger."

Her eyes flared open and he was scared that she was coming for him. He had seen the extent of her temper and anyone that got in her path when she was angry got a piece of it.

Instead of going off on him, she threw her

head back and laughed.

He wasn't sure what to do, so he stood there watching her for a second. "Cree?"

"Life is crazy." She shook her head and stared into space for a minute with her hand on her hip. "I can't believe…Life is really crazy."

"You want to talk about it?"

She stared straight into his eyes. "No. Not at all. He's not worth it." Cree shook herself, seeming to shake off whatever anger and frustration Wayne had caused her. David was glad to see her let it go. He didn't want that worthless fool on her mind all day.

All of a sudden, her whole demeanor changed. She looked down at herself in the dress and smiled, turned and spun in a small circle, slowly and seductively with her hand on her hip.

She walked straight up into his space, bit her bottom lip and then reached up and pulled his face down to hers. She kissed him. Oh, how she kissed him. David felt like every nerve in his body was on fire. If he weren't a Christian man, he'd forget all about Paris and take her up to his room. But he was. So he couldn't.

"Thanks for the dress."

"You're welcome." David chuckled. "Very welcome. You look incredible."

"I feel incredible." She grabbed him by the hand. "Come. Show me Paris."

They went out of the hotel to the train below and got on. Cree had always been fashionable, but today she looked cosmopolitan and international. They sat close by each other on the seat, holding hands. She leaned against his shoulder and sighed. "Wake me up when we get where we're going."

David frowned. "Are you kidding me? You're in Paris. *Paris.* You can't go to sleep. There's too much to see and do today. We'll have to get you a triple espresso or something. I plan to make this one of the best days of your whole life." He kissed the tip of her nose. "And," he hesitated for a moment, taking in the flecks of green in her eyes. He mentally replayed every moment from their past. Scenes came to him in flashes of light. He had to have her in his life. "By the end of the day, you'll be completely in love with me."

She laughed. "Is that so?"

"Absolutely." His tone was sure. "Who knows? We may come back to Paris for our honeymoon."

Cree's smile faded a little. He wasn't sure why. He made a mental note to slow down.

Cree let out a flirty laugh that wasn't as full as it should have been. "We'll see about that."

He stared at her profile as she stared out the window at the scenery passing by. Cree Ann Jordan was a beautiful woman. She was sexy, flirty and outgoing. Unless something had changed, she was a bit of a social butterfly. So it wasn't like she didn't have the chance to meet and date many men. He added it all up in his head. If Cree wasn't married, he was sure it wasn't for lack of men that had tried. She had been raised by a family to get married and have her own family. Why hadn't that happened for her? Why was she single at almost thirty-two? He knew about the so-called black man shortage, but Cree was the kind of woman that could overcome that.

He wondered if Wayne was one of many dudes that had hurt her. Was her heart on wash, rinse, and repeat for pain? He didn't know, but he did care. He could heal the wounds. He was a healer in more ways than she knew.

David squeezed Cree's hand. She squeezed back, but continued to look out the window. David thought about the expression on her face when they were about to board the plane, anxiously looking around for Wayne. He thought of her emotional breakdown after watching that chick flick. He thought of the look in her eyes when she said she basically had no choice but to have breakfast with Wayne, saying they had history. He thought of the anger on her face coming out of the restaurant.

He tugged on her hand. "Are you still in love with Wayne?"

She tore her eyes away from the window. "What?" She wrinkled her face into an ugly frown.

He looked her right in the eye. "I asked if you're still in love with Wayne?"

"Yeah, I heard what you said, but I can't believe you would ask that question." She dropped his hand. "Why would you ask me that?"

"I need to know."

Cree turned the window again. "I stopped loving Wayne Bradley ten years ago. If you remember, I had stopped loving him before I met you."

David touched her chin and gently turned her face toward him. "So he's not going to come between us again?"

"David, what?" Irritation contorted her face again. "Why are you asking about Wayne?"

He found himself getting a little irritated. "Don't act like I don't have a reason to ask. Ten years ago, you left my house to break up with Wayne. You never came back that night. Or the next day or the next. You refused my calls. Finally, two weeks later, when I came to your apartment, you told me that you were back with Wayne, but I knew that already because I saw the woman I loved walking around with him on campus."

Cree shook her head like he was causing her pain by bringing it all up again. In truth, he felt like some kind of a nag for doing it, but he had to know.

"You didn't give me an explanation. Just, 'I'm back with Wayne. I need to try to make this work.' So forgive me if this all feels too familiar."

Cree dropped her head. "Sorry. You're right."

"Before we spend today together, I need to know, Cree Ann. Because by the time this day is over, I won't want to let you go."

Cree took his hand again. "David. I'm sorry. If I could take that day back, I would. For sooo many reasons. If I could go back in time, I would have left Wayne and chosen you. I've paid for that decision in more ways than I can ever tell."

David searched her eyes again. "Then why'd you do it?" The question had been in his heart for the last ten years. Haunting him. What in the world made her choose Wayne over him? Over them?

Cree twisted her lip between her teeth before she spoke. He could feel the weight of her hesitation. "That day when I went to break up with Wayne, he told me he just got diagnosed with brain cancer."

David sat there for a second, trying to process what she was saying. "What?"

"He asked me not to leave him because he was about to start treatment for cancer. He needed my help."

David let out a slow, deep breath. "Wow...didn't see that coming. I...I didn't know..." He shifted on the bench. "I mean I've heard him tell his testimony of overcoming cancer, but it never occurred to me that it was then. And that that's why you left. Wow…" David shook his head. "But…me and you…"

"But what? What would you have done? A person that you once loved is weeping in your arms, begging you to stay and be there for them. Begging you not to let them die alone."

Cree turned toward the window again, leaving him with his thoughts.

What would he have done? Would he have stayed? Would he have given up the one he loved for the one he used to love? If they were dying?

"I'm sorry," he finally said. "I can't imagine how hard it was to make that decision."

She laughed bitterly. She continued to stare out the window. "You don't know the half of it. Hardest life lesson ever learned. But I learned it. And today I was able to put closure to it. Please believe, I would never put another person's well being above mine ever again. Especially when there's no guarantee of anything."

Cree turned to face him. "I'm sorry I didn't tell you. I'm sorry I let you wonder all these years."

David brushed his hand against her cheek. "Thanks for telling me now. And we still have a chance. God brought us back together. We may have lost ten years, but we don't have to lose any more."

Cree's eyes darkened again. What was that

about? "Cree?" He tried to look into her eyes, but she kept avoiding his.

She took the travel brochure out of the side pocket of his backpack. "David, please. Can we just see Paris? Do we have to talk about forever?"

He dropped his head. Was he willing to risk falling for her again, knowing that he could lose? "You know how we are, Cree Ann. If we spend time together, we're going to fall. Hard and fast. I can't take that chance again."

"I don't even know if I'm that girl anymore." Cree bit her lip. "Wayne damaged me, David. I'm just realizing how bad. I'm all messed up inside. I don't know if I can love like that again."

He traced the veins on the back of her hand, visible through her honey-colored skin. "Do you want to?"

She shrugged. A single tear traced down her face. He wiped it away with his lips.

"Okay." He pulled her against his chest and kissed her forehead. "Let's enjoy Paris."

She nodded against him.

They got off the train and walked on cobblestone streets for a little bit, hand in hand. Her heels kept getting stuck in the cracks between the cobblestones and he had to rescue one of her shoes while she clung to him, balancing to keep her bare foot off the ground.

He pulled her into a café. They ordered

chocolate croissants and espresso. She was quiet as they ate. He was afraid to ask what she was thinking about. What did she mean that Wayne had damaged her in ways she couldn't express? He wanted to ask, but it would have to wait. If he got another chance. The way she was acting all fragile, he was afraid she would run away from him again. This time not *to* another dude, but because of him. He wondered if Wayne would ever not be between them.

By the time Cree was gasping in front of the Louvre Museum, the heaviness from the conversation on the train had lifted. "It's like a castle – a beautiful palace." She admired the ancient architecture with statues carved right into the building and then the glass pyramid in the middle of the courtyard before they got inside to see any of the art. Once they did go inside, she was speechless standing in front of the Venus de Milo, the Mona Lisa and works by Rembrandt, Da Vinci, Michelangelo and a whole bunch of other dead European guys she had learned about in her art history class back in college. She was talking a mile a minute about everything she saw and kept looking up at him with pure gratitude in her eyes.

At times, she would stand in front of a painting or a sculpture and stare. Tilting her head and looking, with her lips slightly parted. As much as he was enjoying the art, she was the finest piece of art before his eyes. It made him happy making her happy. She wanted to spend hours there, but he had other stuff planned for the day.

They walked along the Seine River, taking in the architecture of the buildings. Everything was so ornate and grandiose. He thought like he had on his first visit about America being such a young country without such rich history. Some of the buildings were more than five hundred years old.

By the time they stopped for lunch, she was talkative and bubbly again. She talked about everything they had seen, asking him his thoughts on the pieces. She'd ask a question and then talk endlessly, answering it herself. As they ate baskets of bread and drank the finest red wine and then devoured their entrees, she became even more animated and excited. He wasn't sure if it was the combination of the morning's espresso, the wine, the art and lack of sleep that had her that way. He hoped that being with him had something to do with the happiness in her eyes.

God, I want to spend the rest of my life with this woman. He knew that for sure. He couldn't help but think this trip was God's way of putting his life back together. Not just the healing he wanted to get over his father's death, but the heartache he felt every time he thought about how lonely he was.

They went to Notre Dame next. Again, Cree went between flushed and speechless to talking a mile a minute. She talked about how beautiful the sculptures of chimera and gargoyles on the outside of the building were. They looked like evil little demons to him. They were both blown away by the hugeness of the ancient Cathedral. There were statues carved on every face of it. Inside was breathtaking – the organs, the bells, the stained-glass windows, the statue of Joan of Arc. He couldn't imagine how long the whole thing could have taken to build.

After they finished a four-course meal at a restaurant David had Googled, Cree tried to peek at the check. He picked it up before she could look at it. "What are you doing? I told you today was my treat."

She tilted her head and looked at him coyly. "How does a backpacking nomad afford thousand-dollar plane tickets, designer dresses, and expensive excursions in Paris?"

He laughed. She had confirmed his suspicions. "You think I'm broke?"

"Are you?"

"Would it matter if I was?"

"Yes. A lot."

He didn't expect her to say it so bluntly. He had dated many a gold-digger in his day and he was sick and tired of them. If at all possible, he preferred not to let a woman know anything about his financial status until he knew her heart. They had all sorts of ways to dig and probe to find out. He had gotten good at dodging their questions. He wore clothes that were nice enough but not super expensive or flashy and drove a well-kept Toyota Camry. Nothing about his appearance would let anyone know whether he had money or just getting by. No woman ever came to his house unless he was sure they weren't just focused on the bank account.

He turned his head and looked around the restaurant for a moment. It was the first time since he'd seen Cree that he wasn't sure if he wanted to be looking at her. Her answer had come too quickly and she hadn't even attempted to clean it up at all. Most women weren't honest enough to admit that whether he had money or not would make a difference. They would pretend that it didn't and say that money wasn't everything but at the end of the day, if he let a woman think he was broke – which he sometimes did just to see where their head was – it would usually send her running. Good riddance was how he saw it. But now Cree, the one woman he really wanted wasn't even trying to hide how she felt.

"Why would it matter?"

Cree lifted her wine glass and took a long sip. "Because it would."

"Okay, that's good to know."

She flashed a mischievous grin. "So are you?"

"No, Cree, I'm not broke." That answer would have to suffice. He knew his tone was laced with a tinge of temper. He had to admit he was slightly turned off. The Cree he knew was ride-or-die. She liked nice things, and loved to shop but they had never defined her. Ten years was a long time. Had she turned into something else? Something he no longer wanted?

He paid the bill and stood. Maybe it was good that she put the brakes on things on their train ride. He needed to slow down and take his time and get to know who she was today instead of being so focused on the woman in his memory.

Chapter 12

David was less excited about the rest of the magical day he had planned for Cree. But they were there, so they might as well go for it. Her eyes danced with excitement when he led her onto a boat that would take them on a tour of the city down the Seine River. The gratitude in her eyes when she whispered a breathless "thank you" no longer had the effect it had earlier in the day. Now he just saw her as another woman after his money.

When they settled into their seats, she turned to him. "So I did all the talking on the plane last night. I don't know anything about what's happened in your life in the last ten years. Catch me up."

There it was. The beginning of the probing questions to find out how "not broke" he was. He prepared himself to start off with his usual evasive tactics. "I can't complain. Life has been good to me."

She sat waiting for him to say something else.

He shrugged. "What?"

She cocked an eyebrow and jacked her head to the side. "That's all you got? Life has been good to you?"

"What do you want me to say?"

"Something more than that."

He didn't reply.

Cree frowned. "What's wrong with you? You changed up on me all of a sudden. What's up with that?" She tried to take his hand, but he gripped the bottom of the bench they were sitting on. She frowned. "What is your problem?"

David shrugged again.

She studied his face and then nodded. "You're mad because I said it matters whether you're broke or not."

"I'm not mad."

"But it bothers you."

He gave a slight nod. "Yeah, it bothers me that it matters."

Cree stood and walked to the rail. She leaned against it with her back to the water. "David, I'm not a kid anymore. I'm thirty-two years old. Why would I settle for a broke man?"

"Maybe you could build something with him. Maybe because you love him."

She frowned. "You sound crazy to me. It doesn't work like that. Not at my age."

They rode in silence for more than a few minutes with only the sound of other people's conversation and the slightly noisy propeller from the boat. But it was long enough for him to start feeling like a jerk. This wasn't even about her. This was about Felicia and Kelsie and Monica and all the other women he'd dated that had their hands in his pocket. Cree was right. She wasn't a kid. Why wouldn't she want a man that made a plan for himself and stuck to it? A man like her father and her brothers. Heck, this woman was a Jordan. She was headed to a wedding in Kenya and they weren't even Kenyans. She came from something, and she was beautiful. He felt like a fool.

"Cree…"

She interrupted him before he could apologize. "Six months into Wayne's cancer treatment, he ran out of money," she said. "I took out student loans to pay for his treatment. After his cancer went into remission he dumped me for another woman and left me with all the debt. Thirty-thousand dollars. I'm still paying it back."

David's mouth dropped open.

"Yeah, so forgive me that it matters, but it does. I don't deal with broke men. Ever."

If he felt like a fool before, he was a superfool now. What a mess. "Cree Ann…I…" He stepped towards her, but the flash of anger in her eyes let him know that he shouldn't go a step closer. "Sorry. Again…"

"Yeah. Whatever." She turned her back to him and looked out over the water.

He sat on the bench watching her, wondering what to say to fix it. He looked up when he heard her gasp.

She was staring at the Eiffel Tower.

"Ohmygosh. It's real. It's right there."

He laughed, but he was unable to summon up joy. Guilt was eating him up and then something else…anger. Wayne was a bigger jerk than he thought.

"My phone has less than forty percent. It better not die before I can get all the pictures I want," she cried. She took a few shots. "I can't believe I'm actually looking at the Eiffel Tower."

"It's our last stop."

"Really?" She looked like an excited little kid.

"Yeah. Really."

She clapped her hands together and pulled him off the bench and hugged him, laughing. "Wow. I can't believe it."

He had to laugh. He had gotten used to her artist personality and the range of emotions that went with it. She was passionate – whether happy or angry. There didn't seem to be any middle ground with her.

She lifted their hands overhead and twirled around in a circle, like a little girl pretending to be a ballerina, and he lost his heart to her all over again. He needed some sleep because this woman was taking him through too many things.

He ended her twirling by pulling her into his arms. He kissed her forehead and then the freckles on her nose and then both her cheeks. "I'm a doctor."

The shock that registered on her face made him laugh out loud. She smacked him on the chest. "Shut up! Stop lying."

He grabbed her hand to keep her from smacking him again, still laughing. "I'm not lying."

She pulled her hand free and smacked him again.

"Ow! Why are you hitting me?"

"I can't believe you." She jabbed him in the chest with a sharp finger. "Why didn't you tell me?"

"Ouch, woman." He grabbed both her hands. "Why are you abusing me?"

"Because I've spent the whole day trying to figure out how we were going to live broke. Imagining us in one of those tiny houses with our baby sleeping in a dresser drawer." Cree struggled to get her hands free, clearly planning to do more violence to his chest.

"Cree Ann…"

She pouted. "What?"

"You've spent the day thinking of me and you and our baby?" A broad grin spread across his face.

Her eyes flew open. He laughed. "Hmmmm…"

She pulled harder at her wrists, trying to break free. He pulled her into his chest and kissed her, hard on the lips. Her hands went limp and he let her wrists go. She ran her hands up his back and around his neck, pulling him deeper into the kiss. When both of them could hardly breathe, she buried her head in his chest.

"No tiny house for you. You're much too big for that."

"I'm so scared, David." The words were barely above a whisper.

"I know." He rested his head on top of hers. "It's okay."

They stayed there for a few moments, feeling the rhythm of each other's heartbeats and the rise and fall of their breathing.

She finally pulled back. "Then wait a minute. What's up with the backpacking nomad story? Is that what you say to screen out the gold diggers?"

He laughed. He hoped that God would make a way for this woman to keep him laughing until the day he died. "No. I have been backpacking around the U.S. for the last five months like I said."

"Why?"

David pulled back and looked out across the water. "My dad's death was real hard for me. I was the one on duty in the ER when he came in. I did CPR and intubated him and tried to bring him back. I watched him die right there on the gurney in my Emergency Room. I was the one that pronounced him dead."

"Oh my God, that's terrible. I'm so sorry." He felt Cree's hand on his back, rubbing it in small circles. "I can't imagine."

"I had just moved back home about eight months before. I didn't even know why. I guess it was so we could try to repair our relationship."

Cree listened intently. He knew someone who was so close to her family probably had a hard time understanding breeches in the blood, but she was empathetic. That was another thing he loved about her.

"How did it…?" Her words trailed off like she was afraid to ask the question.

"It didn't happen. We never connected. My father was a very hard man. So giving with his patients, but hard with me and mom. I tried to make peace but…" David shifted against the rail. Cree's eyes held so much concern.

"Even though we weren't close, his death did something to me. Made me want to reexamine everything. Myself, my career, my relationship with God. Everything."

He didn't want to scare her away by telling her that his father's death above all had made him decide it was time to get serious about getting married. He didn't want to end up sad and alone. And he needed the right woman. He didn't want to end up like his parents. Married, but living separate lives.

It couldn't be a coincidence that six months after he started seriously praying about a wife, he was standing here in Paris with Cree Jordan. No, it was no coincidence at all.

He looked down at her. "I've got another couple of months before I go back to work. I plan to spend time thinking and praying and figuring life out."

Cree laughed. "Well, if you figure life out, let me know."

He stopped himself from saying, "Let's figure it out together." Even though it was not in his nature, he had to go slow.

They talked some more, mostly about his work. When the boat ride ended, it was dusky. Perfect timing for his surprise for Cree. They walked to the Eiffel Tower and took a few pictures. A lot of pictures actually. Cree did a full photo shoot with a million poses in front of the Eiffel Tower. One minute she was a sexy seductress, the next, laughing and skipping like a carefree, little girl. He shook his head. Just like he'd predicted. A day in Paris with her and he was in love all over again. The last few pictures, he captured Cree yawning. He hated for their day to end, but he needed to get her back to the hotel. She'd hardly slept in the last 36 hours.

David looked at his watch. "Come here."

"Wait. One more picture. Make sure you

catch me." Cree counted to three and then jumped into the air.

He snapped the picture. "Come here, woman." He looked at his watch again.

"What?" She was breathless from all the skipping, jumping, and posing. Her cheeks were rosy and her eyes bright.

He looked at his watch again. "Wait for it…wait for it…"

She stood staring at him. All of a sudden, the Eiffel Tower lit up. Cree squealed like a kid. "Oh my gosh!!! It's beautiful." She threw her head back and spun around in circles. She twirled around and around with her arms stretched out, and then came back and stumbled into his arms.

She looked up at him, punch drunk. "You were right. This has been one of my best days ever!"

He smiled. "I'm glad." Again, he stopped the words that wanted to come out of his mouth. "Give me a chance and I'll give you happy days for the rest of your life."

In time, David, he said to himself. *In time…*

Chapter 13

Cree couldn't help falling asleep on David's shoulder on the train ride back to the hotel. She was so excited and couldn't believe the day she'd had, but the tiredness took over. She had barely sat down and leaned on him and next thing she knew, he was shaking her awake. "This is our stop, Sleeping Beauty."

When the cool evening air hit her face, she felt a burst of energy. She knew she should go to her room and go to sleep, but she wasn't ready for the evening to end. As he led her to the elevator, she pulled on his hand. "Are you sleepy?"

He looked at her inquisitively and shook his head. "Aren't you?"

"Some, but I..." Her voice trailed off.

"You're not ready for the day to end?"

She smiled shyly and shook her head.

He smiled and she felt another layer of her heart melting. What was this man doing to her?

"Okay." He looked around for a second and then led her to a corner of the lobby with comfortable couches and chairs. They sat next to each other on a couch furthest from the main atrium.

Cree leaned against David and intertwined her fingers with his. She didn't even want to talk.

She just wanted to be with him. The whole day she had felt treasured and understood and valued and beautiful and…wanted. She didn't want that feeling to end. She had a thought.

"So tell me about this mission trip that you're going on?" Cree pushed the idea out of her head. What would her family say if she showed up at Brooke's wedding with a date? They already talked about her and all her men. They'd tease her for picking up a man in 36 hours and him following her to a wedding.

"We're doing a mission in a small town called Nyahururu. Preaching and teaching and taking care of orphans."

"Nothing medical?"

"I decided to go at the last minute to honor my father. We didn't have any time to put together a medical component. That would require a lot of planning and gathering of medications and medical equipment."

"Oh…so, the medical part wasn't set up when they thought your father was going?"

"Yeah, well, they were going to, but then they couldn't find a doctor to replace my dad so they didn't plan it. I made up my mind at the last minute."

Cree nodded understanding.

"Basically, I could have done the medical stuff if I'd made up my mind earlier." He cleared his throat. "Let's change the subject. I feel really bad about that."

She laughed. His heart for service was refreshing. He reminded her of her father and brothers. They'd done countless hours of work repairing roofs and flooring in the various homeless shelters around the city. They volunteered their time and her dad even provided supplies when the non-profits didn't have the money. Their current project was Hope House, a shelter for veterans, that her brother Gage operated with his fiancé, Raine. And then there were other Jordans that volunteered. Even her success-driven cousin, Troy, offered legal services to the elderly. Giving was good. David would fit right into the family in that respect.

"Why are you laughing at me?" David shifted away a little so he could her face while they talked.

Cree continued to smile. "I'm not. Not really."

"You've got a strange look on your face. What you pondering, Cree Ann?"

She twisted her lips before she spoke. "Just seems different, you going on a mission trip. I mean I guess it's been ten years but I've never known you to preach or teach or be interested in taking care of orphans. What would happen if you didn't go?" *Stop it, Cree. David can NOT come to Brooke's wedding. You'd never hear the end of it.*

"Why are you asking?" A slight smile tipped the corners of David's lips.

"No reason at all." She shifted back into his side and leaned against him, afraid that her eyes would invite him to the wedding even if her mouth didn't. What was going to happen when they went their separate ways in Kenya? Would they see each other when they got back to the states? She didn't want to think of that at all. She had wanted to enjoy her day in Paris and they had done that. Why did she have to think about what was next?

But she couldn't stop thinking about what was next. Could she open up her heart and let David in? Could she break her 60-day relationship limit and actually do something long-term? He had the things she wanted. Her 4 C's actually felt really ridiculous right now, but he had them. He was beyond cute, he had doctor cash and probably doctor credit, and he had just the right centimeters of height. She loved a tall man and David seemed to be made just for her. She fit into the crook of his arm like she'd come out of his rib. The thought both excited and terrified her.

"Cree Ann?"

"Hmmmm?"

"What are you thinking about?"

"Nothing," she lied.

"Nothing? Come on. You're a woman. You can't be thinking nothing. You're thinking about how much you're going to miss me after we leave the airport in Kenya tomorrow. You're wondering what's next."

Cree elbowed him in his side.

"Am I wrong?"

She still didn't say anything.

"You don't have to say it. I know you want me. How could you resist?"

Cree laughed out loud. "Seriously? Somebody's feeling themselves. So you're irresistible now?"

"That's what all the women say."

Her mouth fell open and she jabbed him in the chest with her finger. "All the women, huh? Any I should be jealous of?"

David shrugged playfully.

She jabbed him again.

He took her finger and placed it on his lips. He kissed gently.

Cree thought it was the sexiest thing anyone had done to her in...well, ten years. The last time he'd kissed her fingers. *God, this man!*

"Anyway," David continued. "Why should you be jealous? We're just friends enjoying a day in Paris, right? What would it matter to you if all the women in Charleston are chasing after me?"

Cree didn't want to admit it, but she was jealous. The feeling creeping up in the pit of her belly was unfamiliar, but still she teased him. "All the women, huh? Okay, playa. I'ma let you and all your women go."

He took her hand again. "I'm just playing with you. There's nobody else."

She sat up and turned to stare at him. She looked him up and down and then rubbed her chin like she was thinking. "Really? Nobody special?"

He held up his hands. "I'm single and free. All yours."

"How is that possible, though?" She frowned. "Why are you single? How come no woman ever snatched you up?"

David looked away thoughtfully and then turned back to her. "'Cause I was never able to get you out of my system."

"Stop playing." She swatted him. "Tell me the truth."

"I am. There's nobody like Cree Ann Jordan, now is there? Beautiful, artistic, funny, full of fire, good family values, a Christian – I mean, you don't find a woman like you every day."

She narrowed her eyes at him. "So you haven't been in love with anyone since me?"

He clasped his hands together and stared down at his fingers.

"I knew it. Tell me the story."

"What story?"

"The story of the one that got away. Or that broke your heart. Or that you almost married. Tell me the story of the woman that put that look on your face."

David stared up toward the atrium. "Why would you want to hear that? Not at all sexy to talk about your ex to the one you're trying to get with."

"There's a lot to be learned from our past relationships. And I don't care. As long as that heifer ain't around now, why should I care?"

"Wow. Heifer?" He chuckled. "So that means you wouldn't mind telling me about your past relationships?"

"What past relationships? I told you…" Cree went silent for a second. David squeezed her hand. "I could say I haven't met anybody worth my while, but the truth is, I honestly wouldn't know. Any sign of my heart starting to fall and I'm gone. I'm out. I run."

"I hope you don't plan to run away from me. You remember I ran track through high school and college. I'll just run and catch you."

Cree blushed.

"I'm serious. I'm not letting you get away from me again."

Cree's heard the muffled Facetime ringtone for Brooke coming through her purse. She pulled out the phone and silenced it. "If I had any stories, I'd tell you. But I don't. Other than everything I already told you about Wayne."

David ran his hand up Cree's back and

reached under her hair to massage her neck. She let out a deep breath. It felt like heaven. "Ummmm..." She wanted to lean back into his arms and never leave. Maybe it was really time to take her running shoes off and let this man love her.

She spoke through closed eyes. "Stop distracting me. I want to hear the story. What was her name?"

"I don't want to spoil our day by talking about Kara."

"Kara...hmmm..." Cree didn't know why, but she had to know about David and Kara. Was it his fault? Did he mess up? Did he cheat?

"It's not a happy story."

"Well, since you're here with me instead of her, I don't expect it to be."

"Okay." He took a deep breath. "Don't judge me. I had nothing to do with what happened."

Good Lord, what had happened? Cree was a little nervous about the story, but now she really needed to know.

"Me and Kara dated for two years. This was before I got saved, so you know, there was no need to rush to get married because of the whole, you know, legal sex issue."

"Okay..."

"She was a good woman. We were in residency together. She's a doc as well." David paused and scratched his neck. "Things started to get serious and I really started thinking about marriage. We hadn't talked about it yet because you know, we were enjoying each other and there was no rush and we were focused on getting out of residency." David coughed and cleared his throat.

Cree was becoming uncomfortable the more David became uncomfortable telling the story. But she couldn't stop him. For him to be this nervous, it had to be bad. She needed to know if it was something she could live with. "Okay…"

"We were pretty much living together – even though one of us was always sleeping at the hospital – but she stayed at my place most of the time. And then one day, she got sick. I thought it was a bad flu or something. Instead of letting me take care of her, she went home. She disappeared for about three weeks and I couldn't get in touch with her, and then she showed up at work one day like nothing happened. Later that evening she came back to the house with her clothes, shoes and toothbrush. Needless to say, I was upset."

David's voice got low and quiet. Cree had to lean in to hear the next part.

"I told her that if we were going to be in a serious relationship like that, she couldn't just leave for three weeks without saying anything. Then I slipped and accidentally said, 'Is that something you're going to do when we get married? Just up and disappear like that?'" He swallowed hard like his mouth had gone dry.

"She looked at me like I was speaking Chinese. Where did I get the idea that she wanted to get married? She went on this whole rant about how men always expect women to get married and give up their careers. I tried to tell her that's not what I expected at all. What she said next almost killed me."

David rubbed his hands together and took a long pause. Just as he was about to begin speaking again, Cree's phone rang with Brooke's ringtone again. She hit "Decline" before the tune got through the first few notes. She switched it to vibrate and set it in her lap.

"Somebody's really trying to reach you. Do you need to get that?"

Cree shook her head and motioned impatiently for David to continue.

"She said that she had found out she was pregnant. She left to go take care of it. Take care of it. That's how she phrased killing my baby. Can you believe that?" Burdened, David sighed and continued, "She found out she was pregnant, moved out for three weeks and had an abortion and then thought she could just come back. She murdered my baby without me knowing and thought that was okay."

Cree felt all the blood drain from her face.

"Who does that? She had no regard for human life. I mean we're doctors for God's sake."

Cree swallowed. David was waiting for her

to respond. She stuttered over her words. "Maybe because you're doctors, she thought...I don't know...she thought about it clinically."

David shook his head. "No, that's not it. That's someone with no family values. She didn't want a baby to interfere with her career so she went and...took care of it. Without even telling me. She was a murderer." David was in a full rant like it had happened a week ago.

Cree was glad he was upset because it took his focus off of her. She was sure she had turned deep green. She needed to get to the restroom so she could vomit. She needed to get outside so she could breathe. She needed to get away from this man and his words. *Murderer...no regard for human life...no family values...who does that?*

She felt like her whole body was shaking. Could he see it? Did he feel that she could erupt at any moment?

He was still ranting. "Really, who does that? Not anyone that I would want to spend the rest of my life with. That's for sure. Needless to say we broke up and I haven't seen her since. I couldn't forgive her. And it was tearing me up."

Cree's phone buzzed in her lap and she jumped. The phone fell onto the floor. She and David both went to pick it up at the same time. It was Brooke again. "Sorry, David. It's Brooke. This is her third time calling. I need to make sure nothing's wrong." She tried to keep her hands from shaking as she pushed the green accept button.

"Brooke?"

"Creesie, where have you been all day? I've been trying to call you." Brooke wasn't usually one to whine, but she was whining like a spoiled brat diva.

"I've been out of the hotel all day, away from a signal. What's wrong? Is everything okay?"

"I'm getting married in two days and you're gallivanting all over Paris?"

"Hold on a second." Cree covered the bottom of her iPhone with her hand. "David, I need to get this." She couldn't stop her hands from shaking as she walked away from him to the middle of the atrium. The words kept trailing through her brain. *Murderer...killed my baby...no regard for human life...what kind of person does that?*

When she was out of earshot, she uncovered the phone. "Brookie, I'm just getting back to the hotel. Let me get upstairs and I'll call you right back."

"Where have you been and who have you been with and what are you wearing?"

Cree tried to put some humor in her voice so Brooke wouldn't be able to tell how upset she was. "Heifer, I said give me five minutes. I promise to give you all the details when I get to the room. That's what's wrong with black people – they just don't listen." Cree was relieved when Brooke laughed. It meant her act was convincing.

She rushed back over to David. "I need to get upstairs. Brooke is freaking out. Pre-wedding jitters. I have to talk her through it." He looked disappointed and she felt a little bad, but then reasoned, what did a little white lie matter? She was a murderer.

David stood. "I understand. We both need to get some rest anyway." He tried to take her hand, but she sped ahead of him toward the elevator.

She made herself slow down. "Sorry. Brooke is usually the calmest, strongest person in the world. I'm not used to hearing her so upset." They stood facing each other. David still had that dreamy, I-love-you look in his eyes. Cree jammed the elevator button with too much force. Why was the stupid thing taking so long?

"I'm sure she'll be fine. And I'm sure you'll know exactly what to say to her."

David tried to pull her close, but thankfully the elevator opened. She stepped on and starting punching the button for the 6th floor.

"Cree, it's going to be okay." Those dreamy eyes that had just held contempt for Kara were no longer filled with anger. He was trying to comfort her and all she wanted to do was escape him.

"I know. I'm just tired. I need some sleep. I guess her calling pulled me back into wedding mode. I've got a lot to do in a little time on no sleep." It felt like the elevator was going in slow motion. She had to get away from him.

Murderer...killed my baby...no regard for human life...what kind of person...

"Yeah, we need to get up early to get to the plane. Do you need a wake-up call?"

Would she even sleep? *Murderer...* "I'll be fine."

They finally reached the 6th floor. She planted a quick kiss on his cheek so her departure wouldn't seem so abrupt. "See you in the morning," she called out as she raced away. His words followed her all the way down the hall. *Murderer...baby killer...no regard for human life...what kind of person...*

What kind of person...

His last words haunted her the most. *What kind of person does that? Not the kind of person I want to spend the rest of my life with.*

Tears began to stream down her face as she raced down the hall to her room. She fumbled with the card key and opened her door. When she closed it behind her, she stood there taking in fast breaths. She wasn't the kind of person David wanted to spend the rest of his life with. Was this some kind of cruel joke? She had found him, only to lose him...again.

Chapter 14

Cree sat on the bed, rocking back and forth. She needed to take off the dress – the beautiful dress that was a reminder of her romantic day in the City of Love with David. She took it off and laid it on the chair in the corner of the room. She didn't want to pack it – it would only hurt if she ever had to look at it again. But then, he had spent too much money for her just to leave it there. She would take it home with her and drop it at the Goodwill in another part of town. It would be a great find for some broke thrift shopper.

She put on the hotel robe, brushed her teeth, washed her face and lay on the side of the bed. She rocked and hummed and willed her brain to be blank and not think. She willed her heart not to feel. Not to shatter in a million pieces. She shut David's words out of her mind. Just as she had shut out of her mind what she had done all those years ago. She formed a new pocket in the corner of her heart and tucked all the pain there. She was Cree. She would survive and just be fine. But one thing was for sure. She'd never try the love thing again.

Her eyes fluttered. She had numbed herself to the point where she could fall asleep. Just as she was drifting off, her phone rang.

Ugh. She had forgotten Brooke.

"Hey."

"Cree, you said you were going to call me back in five minutes. What is going on? Who were you with? Where did you go?"

"Brookie, I love you so much, but I'm exhausted beyond belief. Please, I promise I'll answer every question you want to ask tomorrow when I see you. If I don't go to sleep right now, I might sleep through my wake up call in the morning and miss the plane to Kenya. You don't want me to miss the plane to Kenya do you? Of course you don't. Please Brookie, let me sleep."

"Creeeeeeeeee…" Brooke stuck her bottom lip out. "Okay. It's just that I miss you. And I feel like there's so much going on that you're not telling me. I know you're not okay. But it'll wait until tomorrow."

"Thanks, girl. Please, don't let your driver be late picking me up tomorrow. I want to walk out of the airport and step into the car."

"Of course, honey. See you tomorrow. I love you."

"Love you, too. Tomorrow."

Cree hung up the phone and cried into her pillow until she fell into a fitful sleep.

***

Cree woke up at 5 am, thinking and worrying. She wanted this whole nightmare to be over, but in a few hours, she had to face both

Wayne and David on a plane to Kenya – an eight-hour ride. What if they played the same game and she ended up seated between them again? She would absolutely die.

She had already warned Wayne, but he seemed intent on dragging out interactions between them. Otherwise he would have paid her the rest of her money. What was it with him and wanting to go to Brooke's wedding?

Wayne was the least of her problems. She couldn't bear to see David. Couldn't bear to see the love in his eyes because he didn't know the truth about her. He didn't know she was a murder. That she wasn't the kind of person he didn't want to spend the rest of his life with. How could she tell him? She couldn't do it. She could only do what she did best. Run.

She pulled out her phone and scrolled to his text. It was an iMessage. Good. She hoped he had his Wi-Fi on. She typed and deleted and typed and deleted and typed and deleted until she finally had a simple message.

David – thanks for Paris. It was beautiful. I thought I could love you, but

I can't. I'm too messed up. I can't stand to hurt you again so let's stop before

we get to the point where I do. You're a wonderful man and you deserve more

than I can give you. Please, if you

*have any compassion for me, please,
don't sit by me on the plane. I just
need to rest and get ready to be there
for my sister.*
    Sorry ~Cree

When she finished, she put the phone down and cried and cried. Her stomach heaved with sobs until she was empty. She lay there for a while, forcing herself not to think of what could have been. She'd just go back to life as usual and try to forget that a beautiful day in Paris with David ever happened.

The room phone rang. Knowing it was him, she refused to answer it. She dragged herself out of bed and took a shower and put on her shirt and jeans from the first day of travel. She gathered the orange dress and balled it up and stuffed it into her carry-on.

Her phone buzzed. There was a text from David.

*What could have happened between last
night and this morning??? Please talk to me.
Don't run away. ~David*

She shoved the phone back in her purse and sat on the side of the bed, waiting for time to pass. She wanted to go to the terminal at the last possible minute.

A few minutes later, there was a knock at the door. Oh God, why couldn't he leave her alone?

"Cree Ann?"

She sat there, hoping he would go away, thinking she had already left the room.

"Cree Ann, please. Please, just talk to me. What happened between last night and this morning? What happened?"

She heard the pain in his voice. She was hurting him all over again, but she was too numb to care.

She sat, quiet as a mouse, until she couldn't sit anymore. After half an hour, she tiptoed to the door and looked through the peephole. When she didn't see him, she opened the door, looked both ways and ran to the elevator. She kept peeking and running until she found herself in the airport terminal. When she saw her gate, she also spotted a café a little ways down from it. She decided she would hide out there until they boarded the plane. She'd run on the plane at the last minute and hopefully see neither Wayne or David.

Her plan was working until she heard her name being called on the overhead speaker, asking her to report to the check-in counter at the gate. Her stomach churned. Now they'd be sure to see her.

She thought about it. Why were they calling her anyway? *Please God, don't let this be another delay.* She had to get to Brooke and away from this travel nightmare.

When she approached the desk, the woman attending the computer said, "We need to update your boarding pass."

"Huh?" It was tripping her out that this black girl had a French accent. Somehow she never considered the fact that a black person could be French speaking. She had to get out of America and see more of the world.

The woman punched on her computer keyboard for a few minutes and then reached down to retrieve the new boarding pass. "Here you are. Enjoy your flight."

Cree walked back to the café and sat there until she heard them boarding the flight. She waited until the very last minute. She ran to the gate just as the last people were getting on the plane. When she handed her boarding pass to the stewardess, she pointed. "Just ahead to the left."

Cree followed the direction of her finger and then looked down at the boarding pass. She frowned. 4C. A number as low as four had to be in...

First class. Her ticket had been upgraded to first class. *David.* Tears threatened to fall. She looked around for him but didn't see him. Was he sitting next to her? She stood there feeling confused for a few moments and then she heard his voice.

"I wanted you to be able to sleep." He stood there in front of her looking defeated. "You must be exhausted. The chair lays out into a bed. Get some rest. Brooke needs you."

She stared up into his eyes. "You shouldn't have...but thanks," she whispered. A tear betrayed her and escaped down her cheek. He turned and went back to the economy section.

He had upgraded her ticket, but not his own? She didn't deserve him. He loved her selflessly. She had just broken his heart again and he still spent God knows how much money to upgrade her ticket so she could sleep. Cree put her carry-on and purse in the overhead bin. She dropped into the seat just as tears streamed down her face.

Enough of the crying already, Cree. She needed to accept the fact that Wayne had messed up any chance of her being with David. Then and now. And she couldn't blame Wayne. At the end of the day, she had made her choices. She alone. And she had to live with the consequences.

After they got to 10,000 feet, the stewardess helped her put her chair down into a bed. She put in her earplugs, put on an eye mask, covered herself with the nice blanket that only first class passengers get and fell into a deep sleep.

Chapter 15

Cree awoke to the hands of the stewardess shaking her. She barely remembered the beautiful, black woman with her hair braided in cornrows and perfect make-up helping her get to sleep. "Ma'am, we've got half an hour before we start making preparations for landing. You've slept through the whole flight. Please, may I bring you some lunch?"

Cree frowned and nodded. The girl had what seemed to be a slightly British accent. It was a Kenyan Airways flight, so she figured that's what Kenyans must sound like. Maybe she would stay single and childless forever and just travel the world and explore different cultures – the way people looked and talked and dressed and ate. 'Cause it looked like that married life wasn't going to be for her.

She sat up and gathered her unruly hair into a bun. She took her purse down from the overhead bin. She had to do something with her face before the plane landed. The stewardess brought her a steaming plate of food. "What would you like to drink?"

Cree thought about wine but decided against it. Brooke had said the resort where they were staying was an hour away. She needed her wits about her to start her maid of honor duties. "Apple juice would be fine." She practically inhaled the food. She had slept for seven hours straight and after eating, felt much better. The stewardess brought her a hot towel and she washed her face and put some make-up on. She looked good enough to persuade Brooke that she was fine. Maybe.

When the plane landed, she rushed off, hoping to beat the men through whatever the customs process was. She followed the signs for baggage claim until she saw a man standing with a sign that read:

Lake Naivasha Sopa Lodge
Welcomes Guest:

Cree Jordan

He greeted her with that same British-like accent. "Welcome to Kenya. My name is Kamau and I'm here to take you to our resort. I trust your journey here was good?"

She nodded, but then laughed. The trip was anything but good. When she'd boarded the plane in Atlanta, she never imagined that on arrival in Kenya, she'd be anything but happy and excited... jubilant really for her sister's wedding. But now that she was at the end of this exhausting three-day journey, she was anything but happy or jubilant. She felt like her heart had been dragged across a cobblestone road.

Cobblestone. After her experience in Paris, she'd never see it the same again. How had a trip so magical ended with such despair?

Kamau led her through the entire immigration process with ease. She knew his being there gave her an advantage over the guys and if she could get her suitcase quickly, she could leave the airport and the nightmare would be over.

When they got to the baggage carousel, her bag was like the fifth to come out. God was with her. She pointed it out to Kamau. "That's mine." He grabbed it and she turned to look for the airport exit. She saw Wayne, David, and their large group just coming from immigration to baggage claim. "Kamau, what now?" She knew she was acting frantic and crazy, but he didn't seem to be in any rush to do anything.

He lifted a finger and pointed towards a sign for customs and she grabbed her carry-on from him and started towards it, praying she hadn't been seen. She rushed through the "nothing to claim" customs area and to the airport exit. As she walked through the doors, she was swarmed by men. "Taxi, ma'am? Money exchange? Taxi?" She looked around for Kamau who was lagging behind her. He seemed to notice the urgency in her eyes and sped up. He pointed ahead. "The van is there, ma'am."

As she approached the van with the same lodge name and logo on the side of it, she gasped when saw some familiar faces. "Brooke? Arielle? You came!!!"

She went running towards her sisters. They surrounded her with a group hug and it was all she could do to keep from crying. Just being in their arms made everything better.

"Of course we came, girlie," Arielle said. "What were you thinking?"

Kamau took his sweet time putting her bags in the back of the 15-passenger van. Cree kept looking behind her, hoping they'd get in the van and leave before David's mission team came out. Her sisters looked over her shoulder. "What's wrong with you? Why are you acting like the boogey man is out to get you?" Arielle quipped.

Cree laughed, a little too loud and a little too nervously. She needed to calm herself down. "Girl, just excited to finally be here. Can't wait to get to the resort and see everybody." She threw her hands in the air and wiggled her hips. "Let's get this party started." Both sisters laughed.

Just as they were about to get into the van, she heard her name. She closed her eyes and cursed under her breath.

Brooke said, "Is that…oh my goodness, no."

Wayne ran up to the van. He'd apparently left the group and his baggage behind. "Cree, are you leaving?"

She rolled her eyes. "No, Wayne, I'm going

to sleep right here at the airport. This travel experience has been so amazing, I don't want it to end."

He looked at the side of the van. "Is that where you're staying? That's where the wedding is?" He didn't wait for her answers and turned toward Brooke. "Brooke, great to see you after all these years. Congratulations on the wedding."

Brooke frowned at him like he was crazy. "Thanks?"

"Was real excited to see that you're marrying Marcus Thompson. Congratulations on that. I've been trying to persuade Cree to invite me to the wedding. It would be great to celebrate with you guys."

Now all three women stared at Wayne like he was crazy.

"Wayne, you've lost your mind. I keep asking what could possibly make you think I would want you to celebrate with my family?" Cree stood there with her hands on her hips. "What is it that you really want? And don't play games. Out with it. I don't have time for you and your crap."

Wayne pulled out his wallet and took out a business card and handed it to Brooke. "I'm sure some of Marcus' family will be at the wedding. It would be great if I could get a chance to sit down with some of the Thompson Television Network people. I'm sure you've heard about my ministry. I have a great idea for a show for the network. I'm sure it would be a great blessing to – "

"Are you serious?" Cree practically screamed. "That's what this is all about? You're holding up my money because you want to pitch a show to TCTN?" She let out a disgusted laugh. "You'll never change. A manipulative user to your core." She wanted to spit at him.

"Don't be like that, Cree. It's not just about the show. I told you, I never stopped loving you, baby."

It was one "baby" too much. Cree lunged at him. She wasn't sure what she would have done to him if Brooke and Arielle hadn't caught her arms on either side.

Fear crossed Wayne's face. He knew her temper. "Cree, wait. Let me just –"

Arielle hissed at Wayne. "You got five seconds before we let her go. I suggest you get on up out of here. Fast as you can."

He turned on his heels and left, looking back over his shoulder. Just as he was walking away, David ran out of the airport. "Cree Ann, wait…"

Cree slumped in her sisters' arms. Enough was enough. She looked into Brooke's eyes. "Please, get me out of here."

He got to the van as her sisters were shoving her inside. "Cree, wait. I know what happened. I know what happened between Paris and this morning. I know. Cree Ann, let me talk to you. I love you. Please don't run away from me again."

At the words "I love you," Arielle paused instead of slamming the door. "Cree?"

"Please," she let out a wail. "Let's go."

Arielle looked at David with apologetic eyes. "Sorry, playa." She slammed the door.

Brooke led her to the back seat of the van and sat down beside her. She called out to Kamau who had been sitting in the front seat looking confused the whole time, "Kamau, let's go!"

They drove off, leaving David standing there on the curb, staring after the van. Cree looked back at him for a second, but the numbness was wearing off her heart. She couldn't stand to see the dejected look on his face. She turned around and sunk down in her seat, eyes closed.

When she opened them, both sisters were staring at her.

"That was some serious drama." Brooke said.

"Yeah, Lucy, you got some splainin' to do." Arielle sat down on the next to the last van bench in front of them. Both sisters stared at her.

Cree started to cry.

"Oh, honey." Brooke took her in her arms and held her while she cried until she shook.

When she felt like she had cried for an hour, Cree choked back sobs. "I'm so sorry, Brookie. I'm ruining your wedding week with my drama."

Brooke patted her back. "Girl, I'm marrying Marcus Thompson in two days. There's nothing you can do to ruin that." She paused for a second. "Except be this depressed without telling us what's going on. Talk to us. Let's get this out so we can enjoy the rest of the weekend."

Cree wished it would be that easy. She knew she'd be crying over David for a long while after the wedding.

"We can wait until we get there. It's only an hour drive, right?"

Brooke pointed out the window. "This Nairobi traffic is no joke. You'd think we were in New York City. We have plenty of time to talk. Trust me."

Cree sat up her seat and took a moment to take in her surroundings. After all, she was in Africa for the first time. It was nothing like she expected. What had she expected? She realized that from TV, she thought of Africa as this poor, desert looking place with mud huts and dirt roads and starving children with bloated bellies. This was nothing like that. They were jammed in traffic on a four-lane highway, surrounded by taxis and plenty of expensive looking cars. There were modern buildings lining both sides of the highway. This could easily be Charlotte. The only difference was that every face she saw in the cars and on the side of the road was black. All black.

A smile peeked across her tear-streaked face. "I'm in Africa. Wow…This isn't a jungle, though. This is nice." She held up a fist. "I'm black and I'm proud."

Both sisters smiled, happy to see an appearance of their Cree.

"Okay, this traffic isn't going anywhere. You can take in the scenery once we get on the actual road to Naivasha. You're not going to believe what you see," Arielle said.

"What?"

"Don't even try it," Arielle said. "Two men chased you out of the airport. One of them was stupid fine and talking about how much he loves you. There ain't nothing else for us to talk about right now."

Cree closed her eyes and sunk down in her seat again. She knew there was no way she could explain what they had just seen. Her sisters would crucify her. Where did she even start? Could she even tell her sisters the whole truth about her past? She looked in their faces and knew she had to. She closed her eyes again. *Help me, God…*

Chapter 16

Cree thought Arielle would fall out of her seat when she described her night being sandwiched in between David and Wayne on the flight from Atlanta to Paris. Brooke did a better job of controlling her emotions, but she knew she was just as shocked. As she kept talking, she felt like she should have a bucket of buttery popcorn and a box of Raisinettes to give her sisters. The tale she was telling was more like a movie on a big screen than her life.

She had to pause for Arielle's cussing fit when she told them about Wayne and the money. "He still owes you $15,000? And he won't give it to you unless he gets to come to the wedding to pitch his show?" She grit her teeth. "I got something for him." She patted Cree's leg. "You'll get the rest of your money, sis. Before the weekend is over. Watch – I got your back on that one."

"Arielle, don't do anything crazy," Brooke warned.

Cree knew it was too late. Arielle had that look in her eye. She wondered what her crazy-at-times baby sister planned to do.

Brooke elbowed her in the side. "Keep going."

Cree let out a deep breath and started in

again. She could hardly talk when she got to the part about the abortion. She knew her sisters would be hurt that she'd kept it from them all these years. Why had she? They loved her and they had all shared everything all their lives. She realized how much shame had kept her imprisoned and alone with her pain.

When she finished that part, she burst into tears again. Arielle leaned over the chair to join Brooke in holding her until she finished crying. They both kept saying how much they loved her and that it didn't matter. The more reassuring words they spoke, the more Cree cried.

Brooke pulled a small packet of tissue from her purse. Cree finished almost the whole pack before she finished crying. She could barely stand the pity in both her sisters' eyes.

"Stop looking at me like that."

Arielle leaned the whole top part of her body over the seat to plant a big juicy kiss on her cheek. "Girl, you know we love you."

Cree nodded silently and laid her head on Brooke's shoulder. Brooke smoothed her hair, still speaking words of love and reassurance. They sat like that for a few minutes.

Arielle finally said, "All right, you got that out. We need to hear the part about the fine man that loves you. Stop playing and spill it!"

Cree chuckled a little, but then her eyes

filled with tears again. "That was David."

Brooke frowned. "David from back in college? The one you let get away because of Wayne?"

Cree nodded.

"Girl, Wayne's got nothing on David in the looks department." Arielle cocked an eyebrow. "What were you thinking?"

Cree explained the timing of everything and how it all went down.

"Okay, so what happened on the trip? The man says he still loves you. What's the problem? You need to make that happen." Arielle got on her knees and propped her elbows on the seat bench, staring at Cree. Cree wondered if Kenya didn't have seatbelt laws.

"It's not that easy," she replied. She told them about her day in Paris. The dress, the restaurants, the museums, the boat ride, the Eiffel Tower, the kisses.

Arielle's mouth was hanging open. "I fail to see the problem. If you don't marry him, I will. He's fine, and he's a doctor, and he's romantic and amazing. What's wrong witchu?"

Tears started rolling down Cree's face again.

Brooke patted her leg and glared at Arielle. "What is it, honey? Why won't you let anyone get close to you? Is it the abortion?"

Cree shook her head so hard, her curls

bounced from side to side. "That's just it. I was ready. Ready to open my heart and let him love me. But…" She told the rest of the story about David and Kara. "He called me a murderer with no regard for human life and no family values." Cree sobbed.

Brooke smoothed her hair back from her face as she cried some more. "Honey, he wasn't saying that about you. He was talking about a woman from his past."

"What's the difference? If he felt that way about her, he would feel that way about me, too."

"Cree, you don't know that. That woman aborted *his* baby without telling him. It doesn't mean that he wouldn't want to be with you just because you had an abortion ten years ago," Brooke said. "You didn't tell him?"

Cree shook her head and sniffled.

"So you guys spent an amazingly romantic day together and then you just dropped him without explanation?"

Cree told them about the text.

Both sisters' mouths dropped open again. "You broke up by text?" Arielle looked horrified. "That's so foul."

"Arielle!" Brooke warned.

"Brooke, you know it was." Arielle put a hand on Cree's knee.

"He came to my door this morning. He wanted to know what happened between last night and this morning."

"Wouldn't you want to know?"

"Why are you giving me such a hard time?" Cree didn't mean to snap at Arielle, but she was being a little harsh.

"Sorry, boo. I just…seems like God set up everything on this trip just for you. And you're not seeing it."

Cree blew her nose. "What are you talking about?"

Brooke took over. "I think she means that a lot happened that – if you let it – could give you a chance to fix your heart and finally fall in love. You got to put your Wayne demons to rest AND got some of your money back. You got to reconnect with David and rediscover the love of your life. I think if you give him a chance, you'll realize he loves you no matter what happened in your past."

Cree laid her head back on Brooke's shoulder and let her big sister hug her a little more. Brooke kissed her forehead and it reminded her of David. She started crying again. She sat up to blow her nose.

"Oh my God, is that a…" Cree stared out the window. Unless she was imagining things, she was seeing a giraffe. Like, not too far from the highway, out in the open.

Arielle laughed. "Yeah, girl. Isn't that crazy?"

Cree was more shocked when she saw more giraffes, a few zebras and antelopes. There were large trees, bigger than any she'd seen. She guessed Kamau realized they were finished with their sister session when he started explaining what they were passing. The trees were bottle-brush trees.

Cree was surprised to see scattered cacti lining the highway. She hadn't thought they'd be in the desert. Kamau explained that they were in the lowlands. If they were to travel to the highlands, they'd see tea plantations.

"Girl, these folks drink tea, day and night. All day and all night," Brooke whispered. "If you meet someone new, they want to drink a cup of tea with you. God forbid if you refuse. You'd think you said something bad about their mama."

Cree stared at the breathtaking scenery. Kenya had to be one of the most breathtaking places on the planet. She definitely needed to get out and see more of the world.

The beautiful scenery got her off the hook from any further difficult discussion with her sisters. They stared out the window, pointed and asked Kamau questions for the rest of the ride.

Before long, they arrived at a large wooden sign, ***Lake Naivaisha Sopa Lodge***. Brooke bounced in her seat. "This is the resort. It's not super fancy, but it's beautiful and the service is excellent. We figured since we had you guys flying across the world, we should try to keep the costs down as much as possible."

Cree didn't care. Between Brooke and her brothers, all her expenses were taken care of. She smiled to herself. Things were about to change. She'd send the check to finish off her student loans as soon as she got home. With the money she wouldn't be paying on her student loans anymore, she'd invest in her business, save, and get to enjoy her life a little more.

Cree's mouth fell open. "Is that a…"

Arielle laughed. "I know, right?! The resort is full of hippos! They say you have to be careful at night. They're huge and you can't hardly see them. Can you imagine walking around and bumping into a hippo?"

Cree's eyes widened. "Do they bite?"

Kamau laughed. "Just be careful at night."

"I'll be in my room as soon as the sun goes down." Cree sucked her teeth. "Shoot, I didn't come this far to be eaten by a hippo."

Brooke laughed. "Eaten by a hippo? So dramatic."

Brooke's wedding was going to be memorable. Cree realized that when they pulled off the main road onto another smaller unpaved road. A wedding on a Kenyan safari resort…who would have ever thought her conservative, quasi geek sister would do such a thing? The jeep pulled up to gate of the property. While the driver permitted a security inspection of the van and the bags, she leaned forward to get a good look. OMGosh, there were giraffes, hippos, zebras, monkeys and a mass of unfamiliar birds moving about on the grounds. Brooke had told her not to be concerned about the safari, but she never imagined that was because the safari was at the hotel.

Inspection completed, Kamau hopped back in and pulled through the large, metal gate.

"I guess there's no point in asking you if it's safe," Cree said to him, realizing that he would have no choice but to say yes.

"You'll be fine, ma'am. No problems. The staff at the lodge take care of the guests. Just don't wander at night without security. We don't lock the animals up at night."

They drove in silence the rest of the way up to the main building. The lake had been to the right of them for most of the last leg of the trip, but now situated behind the resort she could enjoy the beauty more. The Lake Naivasha Sopa Lodge was breathtaking. It blended right in with its natural surroundings. The resort accommodations were two story cottages sprinkled around the grounds in and out of the mature trees and lush foliage that had obviously preceded the buildings.

"Let's get your stuff to the room and then we'll join the others for dinner. Everybody should be there waiting for us." Brooke flew through the courtyard. If there was anyone who could outpace Cree in her heels, it was her sister.

She followed Brooke into a two-story cottage where Brooke said the Jordans were staying. The building behind them housed the Thompson family. "I'll be in this room with you guys and Raine until Saturday night, and then well, I won't be rooming with the girls anymore."

"I'm sure you will not," Cree said dropping her handbag on the nightstand. She took in the beautiful furnishings and fought to show some excitement as she prattled on about the unique wood and gorgeous Kenyan pattern on the windows and upholstery. This was Brooke's special time and she was supposed to be excited, but she could hardly manage to breathe. She saw David – everywhere. Her heart was still in Paris.

Arielle and Brook looked concerned. They'd exchanged a few glances between them since entering the room.

"You guys go ahead. I want to jump in the shower and change clothes. If I don't ever see this shirt and these jeans again, I'll be happy."

"Okay." Brooke crossed the room. She pointed out the window to the large main building. "Everybody is there. Follow the brick path. I know you're tired, but please don't take all night. The folks are hungry. We don't have the patience for

Cree-P-time."

Cree smiled at the tease about her tardiness. "I'll be good as new in fifteen minutes."

Brooke smiled too. She reached up to push a tendril of hair off of Cree's face. "Everybody has been waiting for you."

"You might want to come cute though." Arielle winked. "Marcus' cousins will be there."

Cree rolled her eyes. "Girl, I'm not thinking about no man."

"That's 'cause you haven't seen how fine they are. Let me tell you – "

"Arielle, leave Cree alone. I'm sure her heart is in no condition to be thinking about one of Marcus' cousins." Brooke grabbed their baby sister's arm. "Come on, let's go to dinner."

Cree opened her suitcase and found a cute dress that didn't need an iron and pulled the matching jewelry from her small bag. She took her make-up case to the sink. Her entire face looked tired. She'd have to be airbrushed to get rid of the bags under her eyes. And she really didn't care about Marcus' cousins. She just wanted to see her family, soak up some love and feel better.

She took the brick path through a garden courtyard to the dinner area, admiring the beautiful plants and flowers as she went. Everything was colorful and gorgeous. Like paradise.

When she walked in the door, she heard her

name and loud cheers. Cree couldn't keep back the smile that filled her face. There was nothing like the Jordan clan. Who else, with a month's notice, could drop everything and fly to Africa for their sister's wedding? She hugged her brothers and their wives – well, Chase, Drake and their wives and Gage and his fiancé Raine. Cade was strangely alone without his wife. He looked happier and lighter than she had seem him in years, but it was funny to see him sitting there alone and very single.

Her mother pulled her into a tight embrace. "Glad you finally made it. Sorry you had such a hard time." Her mother's lips twitched a bit at the corner and Cree noted a hint of worry. Her mother could see, but she wasn't going to ask why the light wasn't in her daughter's eyes. Not right now. Cree appreciated it, she nodded, smiled back at her mother, and squeezed her hand. "We'll talk later."

Her mother squeezed back and released her.

"Finally," her father's voice boomed from behind her. "We haven't had anyone to entertain us with drama except Arielle. I was starting to get bored." He pulled her close for her special daddy hug. She rested in his arms a few extra seconds. It's true what they said about a good father being a girl's first love. Cree would forever be her Daddy's girl.

She came to the end of the long table where her grandmother sat. "Creebaby." The sweet smile on her face almost brought Cree to tears. Her grandmother stood, but still only barely reached Cree's shoulder. Her hug was as strong and loving as ever. She planted kisses on both Cree's cheeks.

Brooke ushered her around the room and introduced her to a blur of Thompsons. Arielle was right. The cousins were indeed fine. One in particular was a tall, dark drink of rich chocolate. He had the almost-arrogant confidence of a man who knew he was fine and had money and knew any woman on the planet would dream of having a man like him.

He kissed her hand and gave her a flirty look and an oh-so-sexy smile. Cree was sure plenty a woman had dreamed her future Thompson son would have the same deep dimple in the left cheek. Timothy Thompson – she'd heard Brooke talk about him a lot. He was in charge of programming at TCTN. He was the man Wayne would have wanted to meet. Thoughts of Wayne made her think of David. It had been nearly an entire five minutes since she'd thought of him. Five minutes since she'd remembered the look in his eyes when the van pulled away.

Cree reeled her thoughts back in. Last thing she wanted to do was burst into tears in the middle of the family bonding dinner. She met Marcus' other cousins and their wives and a few female cousins. The whole family had this air of richness to them, but at the same time, they seemed down to earth. Brooke was marrying into a good family that wasn't much different from their own. Solid Christian people who obviously cared a great deal for Marcus, otherwise they wouldn't have made the trip. Cree had to fight off thoughts of whether such a fairy tale would ever happen to her.

She took a seat next to Cade. She wondered if he was feeling the pain of his recent divorce in the midst of this family wedding gathering.

"You okay?" she asked.

Cade shrugged. "I've been alone a lot in my marriage. It's not like Savant was always in town."

Cree nodded. Her ex-sister-in-law was an out-of-work, tired actress who was always jetting somewhere to audition for some part she wasn't going to get. Cade did attend lots of family gatherings without her.

"But it's different," he added. "It's different when you're actually divorced. I miss her."

Cree shook her head. "No you don't."

Cade chuckled. "I miss her perfume."

Cree reached for a water goblet on the table in front of her and took a sip. "I miss her shoe game, but that irritable behind personality…whew, I don't care to ever see that grouchy heifer again."

Cade let out a loud round of laughter this time. Cree could tell he needed it.

"You wrong for that," he said.

"You know I'm not."

"She's the mother of my children," he continued to protest, but it was lighthearted.

"She's a mutha all right." Cree rolled her eyes.

Drake came over and dropped into the empty chair next to her. "Ummm...Cree? Would you happen to know where my Beats are? They were on the coffee table in my living room the day you came over to visit Olivia and then all of a sudden I couldn't find them anymore."

Cree plastered on her classic innocent face that always made her look guilty. "Beats? What's that?"

Drake frowned. "I knew it. Common thief. You are hereby officially banned forever from ever visiting my house again."

Cree laughed. "Don't be like that, Drake. You know you love me."

He rolled his eyes but leaned over and kissed her on the cheek. "You probably got hair gel on them or something. I'ma let you keep those, but don't bring ya sticky fingers back up in my crib stealing again."

Cree hunched her shoulders. "Never again." She raised her hand to her forehead and saluted him. "Scouts honor."

"Yeah, yeah, you never did the Girls Scouts. You didn't like being outside," Drake said. 'I'm going to search your bag the next time." He stood and left the table to rejoin his wife, Olivia, at their table.

Waiters entered the room and began placing champagne flutes on the table in front of everyone.

Cree watched as her father stood and walked to a spot that was the most central of the room. "Now that my beautiful, third daughter has arrived, I'm going to say a few words so we can eat this food before I have to go out there and take a bite out of one of those hippos.

Light chuckles filled the room. A waiter handed her father a glass.

"As you all know, Brooke is my oldest daughter. I love all my children exactly the same – "

"You love me the most because I'm the baby," Arielle interjected. She never missed an opportunity to say that. Cree cocked her head in Arielle's direction and shushed her.

Her father continued, "My dear, Arielle, it just looked that way because your mother and I let you get your way. We were old and tired by the time you came along."

Arielle waved a hand and mumbled, "I know I'm the favorite."

Cree shushed her again. "If you don't stop."

"Arielle makes an interesting point about love. Love is a thing that grows over time, so in her mind it makes sense that we'd love her more because we were well practiced in the art of loving children by the time she was born." Her father paused for a moment, not because he'd lost his words, but because he seemed to be overcome with emotion. He continued, "Parents have a baby and they love that newborn, but each year that they love that child, the intensity of the emotion grows deeper. When you think you couldn't possibly love the child any more, you realize you do. Love – true love – is like that. Love is like a tree that establishes roots that get deeper and more intertwined with each year."

Daddy paused and look directly at Brooke and Marcus. "Brooke and Marcus, I know that you have both suffered pain from lost love in the past. Neither of you have had an easy time trying to establish your roots in love. But I feel confident that you're there. You two have everything you need to have an amazing, incredible life together. Nurture your love, every day. Open your hearts and let the love grow deep with affection and respect. Keep God between you and no storm, hurricane, or tornado will uproot you."

Cree's eyes filled with tears. As did Brooke's, her mother's and nearly all the women in the room.

Her father raised his glass and everyone followed. "Marcus, Brooke…I wish you every happiness your heart and soul can hold."

Everyone said their well wishes in unison around the room before taking sips from their glasses.

There were more toasts, and then food, and then dessert, more toasting and finally dancing. Her family and the Thompsons couldn't be more evenly paired in their senses of humor and temperament. Brooke so deserved this after her wretched marriage to Andre.

Marcus spun her sister around on the dance floor. He dropped her into a dip and the passion in his eyes reminded Cree of the passion she'd just encountered yesterday. David. He looked at her the same way.

Cree fought with everything that was in her to keep a smile on her face, but thoughts of David wouldn't leave her. She sighed and for the second time that day, she felt her heart crack into a million pieces and drop into her stomach. She was destined to forever live her life on the sidelines, watching everyone else's love take root while her own heart ached for love of its own.

Chapter 17

Cree slept like a rock that night and woke up feeling well rested. Which was a good thing because they had a hectic schedule for the day. They had rescheduled a bunch of stuff so Cree wouldn't miss anything and everything ended up piled on that Friday. They had family breakfast, a tour of a nearby national park, a bridal shower in the early afternoon, and then the rehearsal dinner with both families. Cree was tired again just thinking about it, but she was excited for Brooke.

It was too early for breakfast and she had too much restless energy, so she put on a t-shirt, leggings and her sneakers. She headed out for a walk near the lake. On the way, she saw some small monkeys in the trees. They didn't seem to be thinking about her so she kept walking. As she got closer to the lake edge, she saw pink flamingos standing with one leg pulled up under them.

She met her grandmother near the lake. She should have known she'd be out there. Grandma Jordan started almost every morning with a two-mile walk in her assisted living neighborhood. Cree wished she could be as committed to exercise, but she was more likely to work out when she had eaten too much for more than one day in a row. She thought of all the rich, French food and wine she'd consumed and picked up her pace.

They walked near the lake, taking in the animals, flowers, trees and every bit of beauty the resort had to offer.

Grandma Jordan stretched her hands up to God. "Who knew Christine Ann Jordan would get out of the country in North Carolina and get to see Africa one day. Life is something else."

"Yes it is, Grandma. It really is."

Her grandmother patted her shoulder. "Creebaby, you gon' be just fine. I got a good feeling about this day."

Cree had to admit she was feeling a whole lot better.

They walked and talked for a while and her grandmother seemed to sense that she didn't want to have any serious conversation. She gossiped about the elderly ladies in her neighborhood and who was trying to date who. All the women seemed to be interested in a particular older gentleman – Mr. Johnson. They fought over who was going to cook him dinner and some even washed his clothes and helped clean his house.

When Cree asked whether her grandmother was sweet on him too, she said, "That old crusty bird? Chile, please." She looked around as if to see if anyone was listening and then said in a loud whisper, "I've got me a young boyfriend. But don't tell nobody else that your grandmother is a cougar."

Cree threw her head back and laughed. Which made her grandmother smile.

After their walk, they headed back to the main lodge to meet the rest of the family for breakfast. The whole wedding clan had already gathered. She and her grandmother had worked up an appetite.

The buffet had too much food on it. She read the signs for the various dishes. There were different kinds of bread and muffins, tropical fruit and scrambled eggs. There was chapati and crepes, potatoes and sausage, some funny looking little beans in a sauce, freshly squeezed juices and Kenyan tea and masala chai. Everything looked and smelled heavenly. They piled their plates and went to a table. Grandma kept shushing away the playful little monkeys that had snuck inside.

When Cree was stuffed and thinking about how she'd have to find a way to walk another two miles, Arielle came up to her, holding her phone in her hand.

"Quick, I need your banking information."

"What?"

Arielle looked down at her phone and typed for a second. She looked up. "Your banking information. What's your account info for a banking transfer?"

"Arielle, what are you doing?"

"Just give me the number. Hurry up."

Cree pulled out her phone. She opened her banking app. "I don't have internet."

"Let me type in the Wi-Fi code." Arielle took her phone and started typing. Immediately, Cree heard her text ringtone chime several times. Arielle's eyes widened. Cree snatched the phone. She saw David's name on the messages. She ignored them and proceeded to open her banking app. She logged in and shoved the phone to Arielle.

"What are you doing? I hope it's nothing crazy."

"Nothing crazy at all, big sis. Just getting you some justice."

She looked from Cree's phone to her phone, typed in some numbers, handed the phone back and walked away.

"Arielle..." Cree called after her. Arielle held up a finger, indicating that she'd be right back.

Cree opened the messages from David.

Cree Ann, you have to give me a chance to talk to you. I know what happened and you need to know that I love you no matter what. Please, we're staying in Nairobi for the night and tomorrow afternoon, we're going to Nyahururu and I'll be out of range. Please text me and let me know that we'll talk when we get back. I love you. ~David

Her heart clenched. What did he mean by "I know what happened?" He had been shouting it after the van as they were pulling off. She read the next one.

*I promised you that I'm not going to
let you run away from me this time
and I mean it. I'm not letting you go. I
love you. ~David*

David wasn't going to make this easy for her. What could she do to get rid of him? Just ignore him? It didn't seem like he was going to go away that fast. Tell him off? Ugh...

She felt Brooke's hand on her shoulder. "You okay, honey?" Brooke squeezed her shoulder. She nodded, afraid of what might happen if she tried to speak. Arielle walked up just as her phone chimed to let her know she had an email message. It was from her bank.

She opened it and her mouth dropped. Wayne had transferred her the last $15,000.

She shrieked, "Arielle, what did you do?"

Arielle had a smug smirk on her face. "I handled him." She laughed an evil laugh. Cree stood and dragged Arielle to a corner with Brooke following them.

Arielle began her explanation. "Your boy has this serious online ministry. His whole life depends on Tweets and people following him online. So I went to his website and his Twitter page and his Facebook page and I made comments...everywhere. Then I sent him a private message, congratulating him on the success of his ministry." The look on Arielle's face was so evil that Cree worried a bit about her little sister. She had always had this vengeful streak in her.

"I told him it would be a shame – a serious shame – if the success of his ministry was compromised if people knew the truth about his past. He calls his "healing" from cancer "a miracle from God" all over his website and pages. What if people know that this miracle was actually medical treatment sponsored by my sister that he doesn't want to pay back? What if people knew he had aborted a baby in the past? What would happen to his online congregation then?"

"You didn't!" Cree's jaw was locked open.

"Oh, but I did." Arielle let out a wicked cackle. "I told him he had twenty-four hours to make things right or I'd go viral on him. I told him we were going to shoot a video, exposing the truth about him."

"Arielle, that's...that's..." Brooke stuttered.

"That's what? Cree got her money, right? That's justice." Arielle strutted away.

Cree and Brooke watched her leave. Their mouths hung open for a few moments. "That girl has watched one too many episodes of *Scandal*." Brooke shook her head.

Cree laughed. "She's right though." Cree jumped up and threw her hands in the air. "I got my money. I can't believe it. $30,000. I can pay off all my debts and invest in my business. My whole life is about to change. Painful as it was seeing him, God really worked it out for good."

"Yeah, God did more than get your money back." Brooke had a serious look on her face. "Not only did he set you to see Wayne, he brought David back into your life for a reason. You have to give him a chance." Brooke looked over at Marcus with an enamored look in her eyes. "Loving and being loved by the right man has to be one of the greatest joys on earth. Don't deny yourself that because of something you did in your past. Open up your heart and love a little."

Brooke kissed her on the cheek and walked back over to the table to join Marcus. Cree had to admit she had never seen her sister so radiant. She had always been strong and confident, but she had gone to a whole new level since getting engaged to Marcus. She looked like she owned the world.

Cree went back to the table and sat down next to her grandmother again. She looked around at her family, laughing and talking and loving each other. She looked over at Cade, again sitting strangely and painfully alone. That would be temporary though. Her brother was handsome and she had already heard a few of Marcus's female cousins remarking so. Cade didn't have the drama she had. Sure he was a single father, but a loving woman would have him, kids and all. And even though he had been married to Savant for nearly seven years, everyone knew he'd married her because she'd gotten pregnant. She had never been her brother's soul mate.

Cree had, however, met hers and it was David. If she couldn't be with him… She let the thought trail off. She didn't want to grow old alone. But could she do what Brooke said? Could she open up her heart and trust love with David?

She looked down at her phone and resisted the urge to text him back. He said they were leaving Nairobi in the afternoon. Could she get up the nerve to text him back? Her heart started racing just thinking about it. She had slept well and gotten some peace walking on the lake with her grandmother. She was enjoying her family. She needed to spend the rest of this wedding weekend in peace.

And David would never forgive her if he knew what she had done. He kept saying he knew what happened, but he couldn't possibly. He probably thought she got nervous and ran after talking Brooke out of her pre-wedding jitters. He had no idea that she was a…

She shoved the word "murderer" out of her mind. She closed her eyes tight and took a deep breath. She felt her grandmother's hand on top of hers. "Creebaby, you ready?"

She looked around. Everybody was getting up and heading to the lodge entrance. "Yes, Grandma." She shook thoughts of David from her mind and caught up with Arielle.

"Where are we going again?"

Arielle looked down at her copy of the printed itinerary for the wedding week. Brooke Jordan was the same wherever she went, even in Africa. Every minute of their time was carefully scheduled and a printed itinerary issued to each family member.

Arielle looked up from the paper. "A national park named Hell's Gate."

"Hell's Gate?" Cree sucked her teeth. "I just spent two days at hell's gate. I'm going back to the room to sleep. I'll catch up with you guys later."

Arielle laughed and grabbed her arm and pulled her along. "Girl, stop playing. You don't get to miss any more of the family activities. It's a park with zebras, water buffalo, antelope, monkeys, and it's supposed to be really beautiful."

Cree frowned as the passed the Lodge's resident giraffe. "I don't know about all this animals out in the open stuff. They don't have any cages in Africa?"

Arielle laughed. "I'm going to see if I can ride a zebra."

Cree rolled her eyes. She wasn't sure why they called her the crazy one in the family.

***

The day flew by. When they got back from the tour, it was time for the bridal shower. Everybody had thought ahead to bring gifts to Kenya with them for Brooke. Because of the conference, it had completely slipped Cree's mind. She shook the wrinkles out of the wrap dress from her carry-on bag and shoved it into a gift bag she had bought in a souvenir shop while they were out. She wrote a note and put it in the bag.

> *This isn't really your gift but I didn't want them heifers thinking I didn't get you something. Act like it's the best gift you got and then I'll hook you up when we get home. Your favorite sister ~Cree*

They had a good time getting to know Brooke's cousins-in-law. They were nice enough and engaging. One of them was loud and funny and kept everybody laughing. One of them was rude and evil. She reminded Cree of Cade's ex-wife. The other cousins and wives seemed to tolerate her, just as they all had tolerated Savant before Cade divorced her.

Cree was exhausted by the time they left the bridal shower. She realized it was jet lag. She hadn't had time to get over all the air travel. She decided to take a nap before the rehearsal dinner. She woke to the sound of a soft voice calling her name. She fought to make out the face in her sleepy state and recognized Raine. She was so quiet. It was hard to remember that she was sharing a room with her. Even though she was quiet and shy, Raine had a kind spirit. And she made Gage so happy that everybody in the Jordan family had embraced her like one of their own.

"Cree, I hate to wake you, but the rehearsal dinner is about to start in ten minutes. Everybody is already out by the lake."

Cree pulled the covers back from over her head. Ten minutes? She jumped out of bed and rummaged through her suitcase. She was glad she had packed her favorite red, figure-hugging, dress that didn't need ironing. She slipped it on with some low, black heels. She put on a light layer of make-up and fluffed her hair. As the maid of honor, she had to pretend to be the bride during the rehearsal dinner. She wasn't too excited about that part of her duties.

Raine waited for her and together they rushed to the part of the resort where the wedding would take place. Cree gasped when she saw it. They had a canopy thing on this floating island. It was the floating pavilion Brooke had described. It was beautiful. The sun had already started to set. Its receding light cast a pinkish glow on the lake. The pavilion was decorated with small, white lights that looked iridescent against the backdrop of the sun.

Everybody was lined up, waiting for her. She stood on the grass, waiting as Arielle and Raine proceeded along the flowered path onto the pavilion where Marcus stood with two of his cousins and his best friend. The music changed to the wedding march and Cree took a deep breath. She was on. Her father stepped up with his eyes full of pride and his chest poked out and crooked his elbow out for her to take.

She glanced over at Brooke who put her hand on her chest, probably anticipating how she'd feel at that moment tomorrow when her father took her arm to escort her down the aisle. She looked at Marcus who also seemed overwhelmed with emotion. As she moved past the beautiful flowers, she had to wonder, would she ever have this moment?

Would she ever get to put on a white dress and march down a flower-lined aisle to a man that loved her with all his heart and wanted to spend the rest of his life with her? Would she ever get a chance to be the blushing bride, without fears and walls from her past? Would she get to start a family her own and hope to have the babies she wanted?

As the music played and she approached Marcus, her father squeezed her arm against his side. "It'll be your turn next, Cree. I can feel it." She wanted to smile and nod, but what if it wasn't true? Her father fully expected to have the chance to walk her down the aisle one day. Would she give him that joy or would she be a disappointment? To him, to herself and to the whole family?

Her father "gave" her to Marcus. He smiled a polite, brotherly smile. The rest of the ceremony rehearsal passed by in a blur. Cree's heart felt pierced in her chest. Was this the closest she'd ever get to getting married? She hated that she cared. Just days ago she hadn't. Days ago, she was resigned to her serial-dating life, but David had changed that. David made her think of love and children and forever. Her soul ached for what she lost.

When the rehearsal was over, everyone was to go to the main lodge for dinner. Cree stayed behind on the floating pavilion. When Brooke and Arielle looked at her with questioning eyes, she said, "I need a minute. That was a lot…"

They both nodded and with some reluctance, left her. Cree looked out over the lake, holding back the tears. If she had any tears left, she wanted to get them out now so that tomorrow, she could be completely happy for Brooke and not feeling sorry for herself.

"You make a beautiful bride…"

Cree gasped. That voice. It couldn't be.

But it was. David Shaw walked that aisle of flowers and joined her on the little island.

She could barely get out the words, "What are you doing here?" She wanted to run, but her feet were stuck to the ground.

"I told you I wasn't letting you go. And you were right, the mission trip wasn't my thing. I honored my father by coming, but maybe my father left me the best gift in his death. You…" The love and desire in David's eyes felt undeserved.

"David…I…you…" Cree looked past him. "You shouldn't have come. I'm…I…there's something about me that you don't know. I'm not the woman you think I am."

"I know what happened. I watched the movie."

"What?" Cree's eyes flew open and the air gushed out of her lungs.

"When you were on the flight to Paris, you were watching that movie and it upset you really bad. You cried and then you weren't okay for the rest of the flight. When you went to the restroom, I looked at the title. And so I watched it. On the flight from Paris to Kenya. I figured it out. I know what happened between you and Wayne. I know why you felt like we couldn't be together."

Cree tried to get past him and run away from

the pavilion. He grabbed her arm, gently, but firmly. "David, please…" She felt the weight of her shame crushing her chest. She couldn't even look in his eyes. "Please, let me go. You shouldn't have come here." Tears began streaming down her face.

He pulled her toward him. He wiped both her cheeks with the back of his hand. "You left before the end of the movie. You were crying and you left and didn't see the end."

Cree put her head down. "What?" She wished she could disappear since he refused to let her go. Just blink her eyes and suddenly become invisible.

"Sanaa finished her therapy and her rehab and got her life back together. One day, she Googled Morris Chestnut. Unlike me, he actually had a Facebook and Snapgram and Tweetybird and all that stuff. She found him. She told him everything."

David loosened his grip on her arms, but still held on to her. "And Morris took her in his arms and told her he didn't care what happened in her past. He loved her and never stopped loving her and that he would always love her. He never found anyone that he loved like he loved her. And he wanted to be with her forever and ever."

David pushed a stray curl away from Cree's forehead. He hooked a finger under her chin and gently lifted her head so that he could look into her eyes. "And then they got married and lived happily ever after."

He planted a sweet, soft kiss on her forehead. "Cree Ann, I love you. I don't care what happened in the past. I want to be with you. I love you and never stopped loving you and I will always love you. I've never found anyone that I loved like I loved you. And I want to be with you forever."

Cree felt her resistance melting. He knew what she had done and loved her anyway. She cried into his chest. He took her in his arms and she let him.

"I told you I wasn't going to let you run away from me this time and I meant it. I want this..." He gestured at the pavilion and the flowered path. "...for us. I want you." He bent down and put a soft kiss on her lips. "I want you."

Cree gave in and pressed her lips against his, tears still streaming down her face. He kissed the tears away. "I love you, David. I love you..." She whispered.

She turned toward the lake and he stood behind her, arms circling her waist, his head resting on top of hers. She looked out over the lake, and the peace of the water seemed to mirror the peace that had finally entered her soul. Her sisters and grandmother were right. Everything that had happened on her journey to Brooke's wedding had happened for a reason. She not only had her money back, but she had unloaded guilt and shame over the worst experience of her life. And now she was standing in Mr. Perfect's arms, being loved by him and him talking about their wedding.

She thought for a second and then said, "I think Kenya is beautiful, but I don't want to get married here."

He turned her around in his arms and faced her. "Where do you want to get married?" He smiled before she could answer.

"Paris…"   they   said   together.

She turned around in his arms and faced the water again, resting her head back against his shoulder. "Wow, I can't wait to see the Jordan family in Paris. They're going to love it!"

She let out a deep satisfied sigh, unable to believe that the nightmare had ended as a dream.

She squinted for a few minutes, staring at the water. She saw a large figure moving across the lake to the shore. "Oh shoot. It's late and the hippos come out at night. I'm not trying to be hippo dinner. For real."

He laughed. "Hippos?"

"Yeah, this is Africa." She grabbed him by the hand. "Come on. It's time for you to meet the Jordans."

The End

Sign up for our mailing list!

Give A Little Love and *Live A Little* available now!

Dream A Little coming January 2017

Laugh A Little Spring 2017

www.sherrilewis.com and www.rhondamcknight.net

Sherri L. Lewis | Rhonda McKnight

Coming January 2017...

Dream A Little

Sherri L. Lewis

Chapter 1

"I totally understand...yes, I wish you the best...Thanks so much for calling... Have a great day." Arielle slammed the phone down and let out a glass-shattering scream.

She had just lost her third major client in the last five months. She only had four left – two big accounts and two small start-ups. She didn't have to look at a spreadsheet to know those companies weren't enough to keep her business afloat. Her financial management firm had started off with a bang, but over the last six months had taken a steady spiral downward.

Not any fault of her own. Arielle Jordan ran her business well. This was all sabotage. Her ex-business partner/ex-fiancé was siphoning off her clients one by one.

She should have known it was coming when she got the same text message she had gotten a few days before she lost the other clients:

Arielle, hope you're well. I wish you the best in everything. ~Lance

Smug bastard. She had ignored the first two texts. This time, she couldn't. She picked up her phone, scrolled back to the message from two days ago and typed furiously:

Hell hath no fury like a woman scorned. Keep it

up. You know what I'm capable of...

It wasn't even a full sixty seconds before she received a reply:

> *First of all, I didn't scorn you. You broke up with me remember? Second of all, you won't come after me. You have too much to lose. I could completely ruin you. So keep playing nice dear Arielle...*

Arielle let out another ear piercing scream and stopped herself just before she hurled the phone into the wall. With the way her pennies were looking, she couldn't afford a new one.

She clenched her fists as another text came through. She braced herself for more mocking, but took a deep breath when she read:

> *Wassup baby sis? How was your date yesterday? Was he smart enough?*

Arielle's anger dissipated a little and she halfway smiled at her older sister's teasing.

Cree's face flashed on her screen for a Facetime call. Arielle clicked the green accept button. "Dang, heifer. You couldn't wait for me to answer your text?"

"Uh oh. I recognize that face. Who done pissed you off?" Cree was looking crazy with her spirally curls flying all over her head. Her face was flushed, making the freckles on her nose stand out. There were tiny beads of sweat on her forehead.

"You been working out? Again? This is serious. Cree got her a consistent man and now she stays in the gym. Who woulda thunk it?"

"Shut up and answer my question. Who got you looking all mad?"

Arielle walked over to her desk cluttered with papers, folders, and sticky notes. It was so unlike her to have everything everywhere, but for some reason, her office space was starting to reflect the chaos her business had become. She plopped down in her black, leather, executive chair. "Lance. He just stole another client."

"What? This is getting out of hand." Cree's nose started to flare but then she bit her lip. "I hope you're not thinking of doing anything crazy." Cree's temper could be fiery, but Arielle knew she reined herself in because the two of them angry together could be dangerous.

"Girl, I've thought of a million ways to get revenge, but each one of them puts my own reputation in jeopardy. It could backfire and then my business would really fail. I can't afford to exact revenge this time."

"And that's the only thing stopping you?"

"What are you trying to say?"

"Nothing. Except vengeance is mine, saith the Lord."

"Anyone who waits on the Lord for vengeance is going to be waiting too long. Plus, He gets all nice and merciful and forgiving and stuff."

"Arielle!"

"What?" Arielle stretched out her long legs and propped her 6-inch heels on the edge of her desk. Even though she worked from home, she still wore a business suit, heels, and full make-up like she was still in corporate America in her New York firm. She needed to dress the part to play the part. Especially with the way things were going.

"You know you're wrong…"

Arielle bit her lip. "I'm not really a vengeful person. I just like…"

"Justice." Cree finished her sentence for her. "I know, but it's not always good for you."

Arielle waved away her sister's words. "I'm not in the mood for a sermon today. Yes, I know I'm wrong, but I just need people to get what's coming to them."

"No sermon…except you should leave that up to God." Cree blew her a kiss. "So is this a bad time to ask about the date?"

Arielle rolled her eyes and let out a deep breath. "As usual, he was –"

"Too stupid to live…" Cree finished her sentence for her again.

"Why are you acting like I'm so predictable?"

"You're not predictable. It's just that I know you. You need to –"

"Dumb myself down? I'm not doing it. If I have to dumb myself down to be with a man, I guess I'll stay single. Anyway, I tried it and it doesn't work. Who I am eventually   comes   out."

"I know. You open your mouth and smart falls out." Cree laughed. "I wasn't suggesting you dumb yourself down. That's impossible. I just think…"

"What? You just think what?" Arielle got up and walked across the room to the refrigerator. Her whole condo was only a thousand square feet, but it was hers. All hers, already paid for. Her brothers hated bringing their children to her house because the whole place was decorated in pristine white, accented with bright red. They were afraid their kids would dirty her thick, plush white carpet or her white, wraparound sofa. Arielle knew she was a little obsessive-compulsive about being clean, but she loved her nieces and nephews more than her carpet or furniture.

"I just think you can be a little..." Cree paused and bit her bottom lip.

Arielle knew she wouldn't like whatever was about to come out of her sister's mouth. She removed a blackberry yogurt from the refrigerator and pulled a spoon out of the drawer. "A little what, heifer?" She knew her sister heard her slam the silverware drawer shut.

"Calm down. My name is not Lance."

"I know. It's Cree and we have very different philosophies about men and relationships. And up until the last three months, you haven't been in any position to give me relationship advice."

"With all the men I've dated in my life, I've got advice for days. And now that me and David are together, I'm an expert. You should listen to my wisdom." Cree smirked. She had recently rekindled a relationship with a college love and had been more than her usual happy self since.

"Whatever..." Arielle didn't need Cree to start talking about David. If she did, she'd never stop. "Anyway, what were you going to say?"

Cree hesitated for a minute, twisting a curl around her finger. "I just think you could be a little...nicer. Your mouth can be a lot. I'm not saying you have to dumb yourself down, but you could be a little sweeter with the way you say things."

Arielle stopped herself from rolling her eyes.

She sunk back into her chair and spun around from her desk to her floor-to-ceiling windows. The commanding, twelfth-floor view of downtown Charlotte made her feel like a boss.

"Men don't like powerful women. Is that my fault?"

"It's not a matter of fault. You know it's true, so act like it. Just try to be a little softer...more..."

"Feminine?" This time Arielle rolled her eyes.

"Your eyes are gonna get stuck looking backwards at your brain if you keep rollin' 'em like that." Cree crossed her eyes and stuck out her tongue.

Arielle had to laugh at her goofy sister. "Why you so dumb?"

"You know you love me." Cree made a silly, kissyface at her. "And you know I'm right."

"I hear you. But I don't know how to be any other way than me. I just have to believe God has a man that can handle a sassy woman like me."

"Sassy? I'm sassy. You're mouthy. Your sarcasm could cut a man in half. Use your smarts to know how to get around the male ego. Now *that's* intelligence."

"Whatever." Arielle looked at her watch. "I gotta go. I have a meeting at my church in an hour."

"Yes, your church." It was Cree's time to roll her eyes.

When Arielle had moved back to Charlotte from New York, instead of returning to the church they had all grown up, where the Jordan family had been members for years, she had joined another church known for its social entrepreneurship and outreach. Her family seemed personally offended that she'd decided to branch off on her own.

"Bye, heifer. Later." Arielle blew Cree an air kiss and hung up. She finished off her yogurt, rinsed the container before putting it in the trash and washed her spoon. She grabbed her iPad and headed out the door, hoping the traffic wasn't too bad.

Tonight, the outreach and social entrepreneurship department at her church was hosting an informational session to introduce volunteer opportunities. Arielle had grown up in a family that made it a priority to do whatever they could to give back to the community. Troubled business and all, it was in her blood.

She made it just as the presentations were starting. Her bestie, Eileen Francis, who had invited her to visit the church for months before she finally visited and joined, had saved her a seat.

"Thanks, girl. I've had a day," Arielle said as she slipped into the seat beside her.

Eileen turned to look at her. "You a'ight?"

Arielle nodded and pressed a finger to her lips to shush her friend.

She sat bored through a few presentations on serving at a soup kitchen, a food pantry and a clothing give-away the church hosted for the needy in the neighborhood. She had done those things before and wanted to do something new.

Another woman presented on a children's program hosted at a neighborhood school where they read to children to encourage a reading culture. They also provided tutoring to elementary and high school students. Arielle loved kids and wanted to read and tutor, but her brothers always complained that she was too impatient when she tried to help her nieces and nephews with their homework. Said she was a demanding perfectionist and that their kids would need therapy after dealing with her.

The next presenter took a few minutes to set up a projector for a Power Point presentation. As he was fiddling with his laptop, Arielle drank him in with her eyes. My oh my, he was sexy fine.

Eileen leaned over and whispered, "What do we have here? Hmmm…"

Arielle jabbed a finger in her side. "You're married. Behave."

"I'm looking for you." Eileen batted her eyelashes innocently. "What are friends for, right?"

When everything was finally set, he introduced himself. "Good evening, I'm Donovan Young and I want to tell you about the DreamMakers Foundation." The first slide had a schnazzy logo and as he continued talking, Arielle could tell the guy was all professional.

Before he started talking, Arielle thought he was the clichéd tall, dark, and handsome – about six feet, two, rich, chocolate skin and shiny, bald head with a strong, handsome face. After he started talking though, she thought him to be a strange combination of geeky and swaggalicious. His heavy, black-rimmed glasses covered too much of his face and he kept pushing them up as if were a long-standing habit and not necessarily because they needed to be repositioned.

He paced across the front of the room in a rhythmless, almost awkward way that made her know she would laugh if she saw him on any dance floor. Arielle decided that he had been the biggest nerd in his high school and probably college, and was still a super geek, but money had given him swag like only money can.

"When we give these women small loans to launch their business, we change their whole life. I have so many awesome stories of impoverished women now being able to feed their families and send their children to school. Some have even built houses. One group of women built a primary school for the children of their village and hired a teacher. They've changed the future of their whole village. Just imagine."

His perfectly tailored suit and Italian leather shoes made Arielle know he was a man who appreciated quality. Every sentence he spoke oozed intellectualism and a confidence bordering on superiority. There was nothing sexier than a smart, confident man. Nothing...

His eyes were intense and his speech clipped, almost impatient. She had rubbed shoulders with his type in New York and was surprised to see him in the basement of a church talking about helping people in 3rd world countries. His "type" rarely thought about the less fortunate.

Except for his smile. When he told a story after story about changing the lives of women and their families in Haiti, Dominican Republic, Brazil, and several countries in Africa, his intensity gave way to a genuine smile that let her know that he wasn't a cutthroat corporate willing to do anything for money. There was a heart under all that serious intellectualism.

Everything about him made her curious...

When he finished his presentation and the lights were turned on, Arielle was the first to raise her hand. She asked about how the loans were structured and the affect of the repayment policies on the businesses.

She almost laughed out loud at the look on his face. She was used to it. It always happened at a certain moment when she was interacting with corporate types. They'd start by looking her up and down – taking in her long legs, her slim, lithe figure, beautiful face – and then when she opened her mouth for the first time, they'd be shocked. Confusion registered on their face as they tried to figure out which box to put her in – "beautiful and sexy" or "intellectual and capable." It pissed her off that they didn't seem to have a box for both.

The corner of his lip turned up in a slight smile as he provided a brief breakdown on microlending in 3rd world countries.

They locked eyes for a second and Arielle almost forgot there was anyone else in the room. Intelligent and fine. Good Lawd…She pulled her eyes away from his.

He tugged his collar and loosened his tie a bit. "Any more questions?"

Arielle raised her hand again. "Will volunteers be expected to do fundraising or grant writing to raise money for the loans and admin costs?" Arielle knew that DreamMakers must have a huge yearly budget. She wasn't interested in fundraising.

"God has blessed us with funding from several private corporations. Fundraising wouldn't be a part of your volunteer activities."

Arielle raised an eyebrow. This guy had

corporate funding. She'd love to know what corporations and whether they could use her firm's services. Companies with that kind of money to give away could be the answer to her prayers.

"Any other questions?" Donovan pushed up his glasses and cleared his throat.

Arielle looked around the room. She couldn't understand why more people didn't seem interested in the organization. She raised her hand and proceeded to fire question after question – each of which Mr. Young answered thoughtfully and articulately. Eileen kept elbowing her in the side, but she didn't stop. Empowering women in less developed countries to successfully run their own businesses had piqued her interest.

After her sister Brooke's wedding in Kenya three months ago, her family had done some outreach in a few villages. A whole new world had opened up to her and she was excited about being able to do more for the women all over the world like the ones she had met in the Maasai village making beautiful, beaded jewelry.

She asked her last question, ignoring Eileen's elbow gouging her ribs.

Donovan Young stood there for a second, biting his lower lip, tapping his chin, thinking. He finally said, "I don't know. It would be great to have you on board to help us figure that out."

The coordinator of the program took the opportunity to step in. "Mr. Young, thanks so much for the information. Ms. Jordan, thanks for the questions but we have to move on. Perhaps the two of you can meet up after."

Eileen leaned over and whispered in her ear. "What was that? Geek foreplay?"

"Foreplay? What are you talking about? I was getting information about his organization," she lied.

"You sure that's all it was? That was hot..." Eileen frowned. "...in a weird, nerdy, superintellectual kind of way."

Arielle kicked Eileen's ankle. "Stop being silly."

Eileen leaned and whispered loudly. "Think about it. He's your dream guy."

Oh, but he was. He was tall enough, handsome enough, and smart enough. He looked rich which was always a plus and he had a heart for the less fortunate. He had mentioned God enough times that he seemed to be a committed Christian. Arielle thought about Cree telling her to tone herself down some. Maybe she shouldn't have asked so many questions.

After the meeting, Eileen made a beeline for the kids reading and tutoring program, just as Arielle knew she would. Arielle sat in her chair playing with her phone. She didn't want to seem overeager to go meet Donovan. He was surrounded by female volunteers, batting their eyelashes, cheesing and grinning all up in his face. Arielle rolled her eyes. Did they want to help DreamMakers or were they trying to help themselves to Donovan Young?

He looked past them and locked eyes with her. He gave a slight smile and an inviting nod. She gave a slight nod back, stood, and headed for the front of the room. As she prepared to meet the founder and director of DreamMakers, she couldn't help but wonder...

Was he indeed her dream guy?

Available Now from Rhonda McKnight...

Have you read the first two stories about the Jordan family?

Brooke Jordan thought her Christmas was going to be boring, particularly since she's stuck working in Montego Bay, Jamaica instead of home in Charlotte, North Carolina with her family. Paradise isn't paradise when you're not where you want to be, but this Christmas is anything but uneventful. Three airplanes land on the island and Brooke quickly finds herself in exchanges that cause love, temptation, and HATE to surface. Will she allow an enemy from the past to keep her from giving a little love to the man who wants to be her Christmas present?

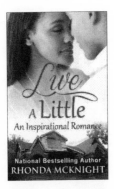

Raine Still has never had much of an identity outside of being the daughter of the old hippie couple that own Hope House, a transitional housing facility in the worst part of Charlotte, North Carolina, and that had been okay with her until her parents died and left her alone in world.

Gage Jordan is a decorated solider discharged from the army after fourteen years due to a physical injury, but the emotional scars are far worse than anything he's rehabbed from. He has a great job lined up and a mass of support from his family, but something is missing and he's starting to feel like it's Raine.

Gage thought his wounded heart had issues, but Raine's pain is much deeper. If something doesn't give soon they will never have a chance at love. Can he convince her to see that "hope" and faith are the balm she needs to heal her hurting soul?

About the Authors

Sherri L. Lewis, MD is the national Bestselling author of eight Christian fiction titles. She attended Howard University as an undergraduate, then the University of Pennsylvania School of Medicine.

After working for ten years as a Family Physician, Sherri left medicine to pursue writing and ministry full time. In 2010, she founded the Bethel Atlanta School of Supernatural Ministry in Buea, Cameroon in West Africa. Sherri's life passion is to express the reality of the Kingdom of God through the arts and sound biblical teaching. She also loves writing edgy, Christian fiction, inspirational non-fiction, and now African fiction. She lives between Buea, Cameroon and Atlanta, Georgia. Readers can contact Sherri at

kingdomartiste@gmail.com or by visiting her website at *www.sherrilewis.com* or use the QCR code to visit.

Rhonda McKnight is a kingdom building, book loving, homeschooling, gardening mom who has written eleven Christian fiction novels. She is the winner of the 2015 *Emma* Award for Inspirational Romance of the Year. She was also a 2011 nominee for the *African-American Literary Award*. Rhonda writes edgy stories that touch the heart of women. The themes of faith, forgiveness and hope mark her stories.

Originally from a small, coastal town in New Jersey, she's called Atlanta, Georgia home for twenty years. She can be reached at her website at *www.RhondaMcKnight.net* or use the QCR code to visit.

More From Sherri L. Lewis

Finding Mrs. Wright

Devon Wright hasn't considered being in a serious relationship for the last seven years. Not since he met Quartisha Shauntae Randall – aka Satan's little sister – who is, unfortunately, his baby mama. He's not the kind of guy that can live without a woman, so he finds himself in a string of short-term relationships, breaking heart after heart – without meaning to, of course. He tells the women he dates that he's not looking for something serious, but somehow, they keep falling for him and wanting something more.

Devon's parents and best friend, Charles, who used to be Atlanta's most *notorious* player, keep telling him it's time to get into a real relationship with the right woman and get married. When his six-year-old daughter, Brianna, begins to ask him when he's gonna get her a "real mama," Devon begins to wonder if it's time to try getting serious again.

When Charles introduces him to the best friend of the woman who convinced him to turn in his player card, Devon is intrigued. Cassandra Parker is smart, sassy, and sexy, but the catch is, she'll only get into a relationship that's headed toward marriage. The more Devon gets to know her, the more he realizes that she's the right woman for him. But will his past heartbreak, crazy baby mama drama, and commitment issues keep him from making her Mrs. Wright?

Becoming Mrs. Right

Shauntae Randall knows she's not smart or talented at much of anything, but she also knows she's gorgeous and can handle herself around a man. So, she's made a career of it. She thought she had struck gold a few years back when she was lucky enough to get pregnant by Devon Wright. She knew they'd get married, he would take care of her and her baby, and she'd be set for life. What Shauntae didn't know was that it's much harder to keep a man than it is to catch him. Now she's lost custody of the child and the child support check and has to go back to hustling.

Shauntae is lucky enough to get herself pregnant by Gary Jackson. She knows she has to figure out how to be a good wife to Gary and a good mother to their child to keep herself in his big, fancy house and his big, fancy car. She has to learn to talk "proper" and say all the right things at the right time. The absolute worst thing is that Shauntae must learn how to be a "church girl."

When issues with Gary's ex-wife and kids threaten Shauntae's "get married and stay married" plan, it's actually God that helps her out. Shauntae decides that instead of hustling God, she might want to get to know Him. But can an ex-hustler really shed her old ways and become a true Christian, and a good wife and mother?

Visit Sherri's website to learn more about her other titles!

www.sherrilewis.com

More From Rhonda McKnight
Breaking All The Rules

Deniece Malcolm is shocked and heartbroken when she finds out her baby sister, Janette, is marrying Terrance Wright, because she was the one who was supposed to marry him! Everybody knows there's a rule about dating exes. Janette is pregnant and not only is this wedding happening, but Deniece has to arrange the festivities.

Deniece's feelings and pride are hurt, but surprisingly, Terrance's younger, sexier, cousin, Ethan Wright, is there to provide a listening ear and a strong bicep to cry on. Ethan's interested in Deniece, but she has a rule about dating younger men. Despite her resistance, things heat up between them and Deniece begins to wonder if it's time to break a few rules of her own.

Unbreak My Heart

From the Author of Breaking All The Rules

A Novel By
RHONDA MCKNIGHT
NATIONAL BESTSELLING AUTHOR

Cameron Scott's reality T.V. show career is spiraling into an abyss. She's desperate enough to do almost anything to keep a roof over her head and provide the financial support that's needed for her daughter and ailing grandmother. When her estranged husband, Jacob Gray, reenters her life offering a lifeline she realizes she still loves him.

Cameron has kept a painful secret that continues to be at the root of the unspoken words between them. She's a woman of great faith, but regaining trust requires telling all and healing old wounds that she believes would destroy any chance for happiness they could have.

Jacob Gray believed he'd spend the rest of his life loving his wife, that is until he discovered she was pregnant and there was no way it could be his child. He tried to put Cameron out of his mind and heart, but five years have passed and he still loves her. Jacob risks everything, including his fortune, in hopes of getting a second chance at love. Though he quickly discovers Cameron's not interested in rekindling what they had years ago.

Will Jacob convince her to forgive the mistakes in their past and allow each other to heal their broken hearts?

Visit Rhonda's website to learn about her other titles!

www.rhondamcknight.net

Made in the USA
Middletown, DE
03 June 2018